Heart of the Texas Doctor

Heart of the Texas Doctor

A Heart of Texas Romance

Eve Gaddy

TULE
PUBLISHING

Chapter One

"MATCHMAKER AT TWO o'clock," Turner McBride said to his brother Graham.

"Damn. Maybe if I don't make eye contact she'll go away."

"Doubtful. She's headed this way."

Clara Perkins, aka *the Matchmaker*, was a nice older lady but for reasons unclear to Graham, she'd made it her mission in life to find him a girl. Him and his brothers, Turner and Spencer. But since he was the oldest of the McBride brothers, she was focused on him. He could hear her saying in her little-old-lady Texas drawl, "It's criminal that a man—a doctor yet—of your age is still single. I've got just the girl for you."

This was the latest in a seemingly endless line of women she'd introduced to Graham. Every one of them had been *just the girl* for him. At first he'd fought it, but eventually he gave up. It was easier to make a date than to deal with Clara's disappointment if he didn't. If they liked each other, fine. If not, it was one date. Most of the women were nice and he'd enjoyed them, but Clara had also picked a few real stinkers.

"Who is it this time?" he asked his brother, still with his

back to the women.

"You're in luck. Clara's got Bella Benson with her."

"Bella Benson? Oh, the one who owns Bella's Salon on Main Street?" Last Stand was a small town, so he knew who she was, but they'd never actually met.

"That's the one. Don't worry, though." Turner gave him a smart-ass grin. "I imagine you're too old for her," he said before deserting him.

"Chicken," Graham muttered under his breath. Graham didn't particularly like parties. He couldn't stand to make small talk, which was also one of his problems with blind or arranged dates. It was hard to have a decent conversation with a woman you hardly knew. Nine times out of ten, if he didn't bring a date, he'd get cornered by someone wanting to set him up with yet another woman. And he didn't want to ask a woman out simply to discourage the matchmakers. It made him feel like a wuss.

But Minna Herdmann's birthday bash was a command performance. Every year on April 7, Last Stand, Texas, hosted a birthday party for its oldest resident. This was the seventh year the one-hundred-two-year-old matriarch had been honored in that manner. Everyone in town was invited and most of them attended or at least dropped in to wish Minna happy birthday.

"Graham," he heard Clara call out.

Resigned, Graham turned around to greet Clara and her latest protégé. He could always pretend to get a call from the hospital. After all, no one needed to know that he wasn't actually on call today.

And then he saw her. Momentarily dumbstruck, Graham stared at the vision standing in front of him. Her blonde hair was long, falling well past her shoulders, with part of it pulled back in a braid with gold beads threaded through it. And it was streaked with rainbow colors. Rainbows. Pastel colors of turquoise, pink, purple, pale green, blue, and of course, blonde. It should have been hideous, or at the least, strange, but it wasn't. Oddly enough, it suited her. But then, she was a good ten years or more younger than him and very pretty, to boot.

Then he realized Clara had the identical hairstyle and dye job, except her hair was pale silver and not as long. And streaked with rainbow colors. Wow.

At least they weren't dressed alike.

Clara wore a pink dress with ice cream cones on it. Large ice cream cones.

Bella wore a sleeveless rainbow-colored minidress in the same pastel colors as her hair, turquoise cowboy boots on her feet and lots of bangles on her arms. She looked good. No, she looked hot. The thought disconcerted him a little but there was no denying that from the tips of her rainbow-colored hair to the soles of her fancy turquoise cowboy boots, Bella Benson was smokin'.

"Graham, here's someone I want you to meet," Clara said.

His gaze collided with Bella's. She didn't look nervous or ill at ease. Maybe she was as accustomed as he was to Clara's machinations. She smiled at him. Damn, she had a dynamite smile. Why had he never really noticed her before?

Because she's way too young for you, dumbass.

"Mrs. Perkins, how are you?" he asked, managing to collect himself.

"Now, Graham, you know I've asked you to call me Clara a million times. And I'm as fine as can be expected at my age. Though Minna's got several years on me and look at her," she said, waving a hand in the honoree's direction. The matriarch sat under a huge awning on the patio of the Carriage House restaurant, also one of the oldest fixtures of Last Stand. Minna waved back, in the regal, old-fashioned way she had, prompting a smile from Graham. She wore a pale blue dress and her silver hair was braided and wrapped around her head in a style that had no doubt been popular almost a century ago when Minna was a young woman.

Taking Bella's arm, Clara tugged her forward. "Bella, this is Graham McBride. He's a doctor at the hospital. He's a fancy kind of specialist. Something to do with hearts. Graham," she continued, "this is Bella Benson. She owns the beauty shop on Main."

"It's nice to meet you," Graham said, offering his hand.

She took his hand in a firm grip and smiled that beautiful smile again. Her eyes were brown. Luscious, chocolate brown, like that of a sweeter-than-sin candy bar. "Nice to meet you, too."

Her voice was husky, with more of a drawl than a twang. He was intrigued, and growing more so, in spite of his irritation at being railroaded by Clara once again.

"I'm going to talk to Minna," Clara announced. "Bella, you're a sweetheart. It's been fun being twins," she said with a twinkle in her faded blue eyes. "I may be back in before long to have you do something permanent in the color department."

"Any time, Clara." She smiled at the older lady and watched her go. Then she turned to Graham and said, "Number fourteen."

Graham blinked. "Excuse me?" What the hell did that mean?

"You're the fourteenth man Clara's introduced me to. And judging from your expression when you first turned around, I'm guessing I'm about number forty-five of the women she's introduced to you."

He stared at her for a minute, then threw back his head and laughed. "I didn't realize I was so obvious. As to the number, I stopped counting a long time ago."

"Ah, but you've known her longer than I have."

"True. Clara was one of my father's patients before he retired." He steered her toward a table, guiding her away from the center of the patio.

The Carriage House, both indoors and out, was decked out in balloons, streamers, flowers and Texas memorabilia. Chairs and tables of all sizes were spread out over the flagstone patio, and music played softly from outdoor speakers. Graham congratulated himself on scoring one of the last remaining tables with a little shade.

"You realize Clara is going to immediately announce to all her friends that she is the matchmaker supreme," Bella said, taking a seat.

"No harm in that." Not exactly true. If Clara thought

she'd finally found him a girl he liked, he'd never live it down. Then again, maybe she'd quit throwing women at him.

Bella nodded in Clara's direction. "She's already at it. See her talking to Mrs. Herdmann?"

"Mrs. H is the guest of honor. That doesn't mean they're talking about—" He broke off as both ladies turned to stare right at them with wide smiles. Clara even winked.

Bella laughed. "Don't worry. They'll forget all about us once they realize we aren't going out together."

"You're probably right," he said. "But what if we do go out together?"

Bella crossed her legs, showing a stretch of shapely, tanned leg when her dress rode up a little. "Why, are you asking me out?"

"Yes," he said. "Can I take you to dinner Saturday night?"

"That depends."

"On what?"

"Are you asking because you want to go out with me? Or are you asking because it's easier to go along with Clara than to fight her?"

❦

GRAHAM STARED AT her for a moment before laughing. "Nailed that one, didn't you?"

Well, crap. Bella knew it was too good to be true. She'd finally gotten to meet Graham McBride. The man she'd been crushing on for the last several months. And she hadn't even had to do anything. Clara Perkins had arranged it, not even realizing that for once she'd found someone Bella might actually be interested in.

Who apparently had no real interest in her. Damn it.

"That's often the case when Clara introduces a woman to me," Graham continued. "But not this time."

Bella lifted an eyebrow. "Nice try. Why should I believe this is any different from the other ninety-five times Clara maneuvered you into asking someone out?"

"Not ninety-five," he protested. "I thought we'd agreed it's closer to forty-five. And it's different because you're different."

"Thanks, I think." She might have a crush on him but that didn't mean she was stupid. He was obviously smooth, and just as plainly nice. Otherwise, why would he go along with Clara? Much as she'd like to get to know him, she didn't want him to ask her out simply because he didn't want to hurt her—or Clara's—feelings.

Graham was smiling at her with a lady-killer smile she'd always heard about but hadn't known really existed until this moment. *Damn, this guy is dangerous.* Unlike a number of men she knew, Graham kept his eyes focused on her face instead of her chest.

"I like your hair," he said.

"My hair?"

"Yeah, it's pretty. Different."

"I'm a hair stylist. I change my hair color as often as I change outfits." She thought about that a minute and added,

"Okay, not quite as often." Bella caught sight of her friends: Delilah Corbyn and Joey Douglas. They both gave her a knowing smile and a thumbs-up sign, which—thankfully—Graham couldn't see. That was the problem with best friends. They knew all your secrets.

"Would you like a drink?" Graham asked. "There's non-alcoholic punch, wine, and beer. And soft drinks, I'm sure."

"How about a beer?"

"Will do," he said. "I'll be right back."

Graham McBride, make that *all* the McBride men, were the subject of many a conversation in her salon. Even though prior to this Bella had only seen Graham from a distance, she'd always thought he was hot. The closest she'd been to him in person was in line several people behind him at *Char-Pie*, the pie bakery on Main. He'd been in scrubs with his hospital ID clipped on the shirt pocket, and he looked very professional. Now, in jeans and boots and a baby-blue button-down shirt, the man was heart-breakingly gorgeous. Dark brown hair, cut short, in a style that told her he was a patron of the barbershop in town that had been around forever. His eyes were a clear green, with hazel turning to brown around the irises, and framed with ridiculously long, dark lashes. He had a strong jaw, clean-shaven at the moment, a straight nose with a slight bump at the bridge suggesting he'd broken it at some point, and a mouth that was frankly sensuous.

"And what have we here? How does the object of your fantasies hold up in real life?" Delilah asked.

"Nosy friends want to know," Joey added.

"I thought the phrase was inquiring minds want to know?" Bella said.

"It is. But Delilah and I are just nosy."

They all laughed. "Have a seat," Bella said. "Graham's gone to get us a couple of beers."

"Did he ask you out?" Joey asked as she pulled out a chair.

"Clara introduced us. Of course he asked me out." Delilah and Joey knew all about Clara's crusade to find Bella a man.

"Good point. Where are you going and when?" Delilah asked, taking the other seat.

"I don't know. I haven't agreed to go."

"Why the heck not?" Delilah asked.

"I don't want to go if he only asked me out because Clara will bug him to death if he doesn't."

"This is the man you've been crushing on for months," Joey reminded her. "He asked you out. You should go."

Graham had reappeared on the patio but he'd stopped to talk to a woman. A very pretty woman. After a brief conversation, he turned and looked straight at Bella, smiled and started walking toward her, carrying two beers.

"Oh." Delilah placed her hand over her heart and patted it. "Be still my beating heart."

"Graham can probably help you with that," Bella said. "After all, he is a heart surgeon."

Joey stifled a laugh as they both got up.

"You don't have to leave," Bella said.

Graham arrived with the beers just then and set them

down. Before Bella could introduce him to her friends, he offered his hand saying, "I'm Graham McBride. I don't think we've met."

Joey and Delilah introduced themselves and left very shortly after that despite Graham asking them to stick around.

Graham sat down and said, "So what's the verdict?"

"The verdict?"

"Yes." He gestured at the two women. "Are you going out with me or not?"

"What do my friends have to do with that?"

"A lot, I imagine." She stared at him and he added, "I have a mother, a sister, and an ex-wife. They all have girlfriends and their girlfriends' opinions matter to them."

"True. But we only pay attention if we agree with that opinion."

Graham laughed. "You still haven't answered my question. Are you going to let me take you to dinner Saturday night?"

Just say yes. You know you want to. "I'd love to go to dinner with you, but Saturday night could be a problem."

"Why is Saturday a problem?" he asked.

"Are you kidding? Have you forgotten the Bluebonnet Festival is next weekend?"

He looked completely blank for a minute. "The Bluebonnet Festival? Oh, right. I'm usually working that weekend. But since I'm off, it slipped my mind."

She didn't see how one of Last Stand's biggest events could have "slipped his mind" but clearly it had. "Don't you like the festival?" she asked curiously.

"Honestly, I haven't been in years."

"By choice?"

"Not exactly. Like I told you, usually I'm working." He took a drink and set down his bottle.

"But you don't hate it or anything like that?"

"Of course I don't hate it. Why would I hate it?"

"I don't know. Maybe you don't like crowds."

"Crowds don't bother me. Now that I think about it, my sister is riding one of her mustangs in the parade."

"She does that every year. You should try to watch it."

"Maybe I will."

"Since you're free, why don't we meet later on at the festival? We can grab some food there. There'll be tons of stuff to eat and drink, and all sorts of things to do. I won't be totally free until later in the afternoon, though. I'll be minding my booth in the park."

"That sounds like a great idea." He took another sip of his beer. "Tell me, Bella, what will you do at your booth?"

"Braid hair and/or put temporary color on it. It's a big hit with kids. Both girls and boys. Some of the moms, too."

"What about the dads?"

She laughed. "Them, not so much."

"Where and when should I meet you?"

"Meet me at my booth in the park around four," she said, mentioning the approximate location of her booth.

"Great. It's a date then." He smiled at her and she realized with a shock that he had dimples.

Oh, Lord, dimples were one of her weaknesses. *Get a*

hold of yourself, Bella. He asked you for one date. One. To steady herself she took a drink.

"You seem awfully young to own your own business. You've only been here in Last Stand a few years, haven't you?"

"Yes, three years, earlier this spring. I've been on my own since I was seventeen, so I don't feel all that young. But as it happens, a few years ago I inherited the property from a relative I didn't know I had. It used to be an antique shop but by the time it came to me, it had been closed for years. I turned it into a hair salon."

"Where were you before you moved here?"

"Houston. Before that Austin. Before that Dallas. Before that Fort Worth."

"I get the feeling you moved around a lot."

"How did you guess?"

They both laughed.

Graham took a drink of his beer. "What do—?"

She heard tires squealing and horns blaring. Then a tremendous crash and the sound of glass shattering. Bella looked at Graham, saying, "That sounded like a—"

But Graham was already up and moving toward the street. Bella got up and raced after him.

Chapter Two

TIRES SCREECHING, HORNS blaring, then the clang and crash of metal on metal and the unmistakable sound of glass shattering. *A wreck. A bad one from the sound of it.* Graham ran out the open gate of the patio and looked in the direction he thought the noise had come from. Across the street and to his left he saw Shane Highwater, Last Stand's police chief, heading in a dead run toward an upside-down truck in front of the library. A step behind him and headed in the opposite direction was his brother, Sean, a Last Stand police detective. He wasn't surprised two lawmen were the first to arrive on the scene. In fact, he'd have been surprised if they hadn't.

Directly across the street from the Carriage House there was a small bus—a tour bus—which had crashed into the window of *Verflucht*, August Wolf's tasting room that had yet to open. The truck and the bus must have collided, sending the bus into the building and the truck to rest in front of Asa Fuhrmann's statue. The noise from the crash had hardly faded when he heard an explosion. He whipped around and saw that the wrecked truck had burst into flames. He started toward it but the chief shouted, "Doc!

Only room for one there. I've got it. Take the bus, and the building."

He hesitated but he knew the chief could handle himself in an emergency. He glimpsed Sean disappearing into the wrecked bus. He nodded at the chief and headed in the bus's direction.

As he reached the building, someone came running up behind him but went toward the building rather than the bus. Axel Wolf, he realized, thankfully. Axel was a volunteer paramedic so he'd be able to take care of any injuries in the building. "Call me if you need an extra pair of hands," he told Axel. "I'll be here in the bus."

"Will do," Axel said and disappeared into the building.

The bus's front end was wedged into Verflucht's big picture window looking out over Main. He hoped Axel didn't find anyone too badly injured inside the store, but right now his main concern was the people on the bus. Graham vaulted up the stairs, taking them in one step, and as he did people began talking, crying and asking what had happened. He swept the bus with a critical gaze, looking for the most serious injuries. The first person he saw was the driver, a local named Marianne Wright, bleeding and wedged between her seat and the deployed airbag.

Sean had already begun assessing injuries. "Check the driver, Doc," he said when he saw Graham. "She's hurt but was conscious and talking. I tried to take care of her but she wouldn't let me. She told me to go see about her passengers."

Marianne, though awake and aware, was clearly dazed. "The truck just came out of nowhere. I never saw it until it hit us," she said in a bewildered tone. "How are the passengers?"

"Sean's taking care of them. Let's deal with you and then I'll help Sean."

She moaned pitifully. "I'm so glad you're here, Dr. McBride. I'm hurting pretty bad."

Quickly, Graham pulled out his pocketknife and cut the bag loose. The airbag had caused some facial contusions and likely a lot of bruising. He wouldn't know more until he could check her more closely. "Let's get you out of here." Graham unhooked her seat belt, then took her right arm to help her out of the seat.

She gave a cry of pain and said, "My arm." She clutched her left arm, cradling it against her body. "I think it's broken."

Graham checked her arm, careful not to move it too much. It lay at an unnatural angle against her side. "I think you're right. The paramedics will be here soon and they'll take care of you. In the meantime let me—"

"What can I do?" Bella asked, poking her head in the doorway.

"Bella! I'm glad you're here. Help Marianne out. Careful of her left arm. It could be broken. See if you can find a paramedic."

"Will do."

"Was anyone in the building? Do you know?"

"I'm afraid so," Bella said. "I heard the vintner, the vineyard manager and August Wolf were all inside. I'll check and let you know who was hurt and if they need more hands as soon as I help this lady."

Bella took over, talking soothingly to Marianne as she led her away. Other people were getting off the bus as Sean sent the uninjured to the park and the ones with minor injuries across the street to the Carriage House. Graham started checking people on the other side of the bus, but thankfully the injuries were minor and he sent them on their way.

Bella came back and said, "August wasn't hurt but the other two have injuries. I don't know how bad. Axel says to tell you he's got help and they can handle it until the other paramedics get here."

"Thanks."

"I've been sending the people who are bleeding or complaining of pain across the street to the Carriage House. The others, I've been sending to the park."

"Good, that's what Sean and I told them too."

"There are a bunch of looky-loos as well. It's hard to tell the difference between them and the people who need help."

"Not surprising."

"Anything else you want me to do?" she asked.

"Not right now."

"Okay, I'll check back."

Obviously, Bella was capable in an emergency. Which was good since he knew not everyone was. He returned to assessing injuries.

"Graham," Sean said from the back. "I need you here."

Something in his voice, not to mention his request for help, told Graham that whatever had happened it wasn't good.

He left the people he was checking with a hasty, "I'll be back," and went to Sean. "What is it?"

Sean indicated a man slumped over into the seat beside him, which was empty. "I can't get a pulse," he said in an undertone.

Graham laid his fingers on the man's neck, then put his ear to his mouth. No pulse. No breathing sounds. "We need to get him outside, stat."

Sean, who had opened up the doors while Graham was evaluating the man, said, "Let's take him out the rear." He took the man's feet and Graham took his head.

"Cardiac arrest," he told Sean in a low voice. Not that keeping quiet mattered since everyone would soon see that they were performing CPR. Graham knew the Last Stand PD required the officers to keep up their certification, so he'd have someone to help. They carried the man a short distance to a grassy area between buildings and laid him flat on the ground. Sean pushed up his shirt to allow Graham free access to the man's chest. Graham placed a palm on his bare chest, interlaced his fingers, and began compressions. Sean went to his head, ready to begin breathing when Graham stopped. They completed two cycles of breathing and compressions and Graham asked, "Is there a defibrillator on the bus?"

"No, but we have one at the PD. I'll go—"

Sean broke off as Bella ran up and said, rather breathlessly, "The police department had a defibrillator if you need it." She set a red case down beside them.

"We do. Thanks." He didn't stop to wonder how she'd

known so quickly; he was just glad she had. Sean opened the case and handed the pads to Graham then turned on the machine. Graham placed the pads on the man's chest and sat back, waiting for the machine to take over. This was one of the newer automated external defibrillators designed for a layman to operate, so it gave voice instructions and operated pretty much automatically.

Graham and Sean drew back when the machine instructed them to "Clear. Analyzing." Following the voice instructions, Graham alternated doing compressions with the machine instructing him to stand clear and administering a shock. Sean and Bella stood by, ready to help.

After a couple of cycles of CPR and shock the machine announced, "Pulse detected. Continue compressions."

"Great," Graham said, relief spreading through him. He continued CPR, wondering when the paramedics would arrive.

"Thank God," Bella said.

"Is everyone off the bus?" Graham asked after a moment.

"No," Sean said.

"Go," Graham told him. "The paramedics should be here soon. The sirens sound close."

Sean hesitated a moment, then nodded and took off.

Sure enough, a couple of minutes later Graham heard his brother Spencer's voice. Spencer was the rebel of the family. During the Texas Revolution, the original Doc McBride took care of the wounded during the battle of Last Stand, for which the town was named. From that time on, the family had always had at least one doctor in a generation. Spencer said that Graham and Turner could carry on that tradition. He'd become a firefighter and paramedic rather than an M.D.

"What's happening here?"

"Cardiac arrest," Graham told him. "I've been doing CPR since we found him in the bus and we used the AED after the first cycle of CPR. He's got a pulse now."

"Good." The other paramedic took over for Graham. "We'll take care of him," Spencer told him.

Graham nodded, glad of it since the emergency team would have everything they needed to give the man the proper care, especially if he arrested again. "Spencer, do you know what happened to the people in the truck?"

Spencer looked grim. "Two dead at the scene. One in critical condition, thanks to the chief who pulled him out, or he'd be dead too. He's en route to the hospital."

"Damn. What about the building? I heard two people inside were hurt."

"Yes, but I don't know the extent of the injuries since I was with the burn victim."

"Okay. I'll find out more when I get to the hospital. I'm going to see if Sean needs more help and then I'll head over there."

"Thank you for bringing the defibrillator," he said to Bella, watching the EMTs load the patient into the ambulance. "How did you know we needed it?"

"You laid the man out flat on the ground and started chest compressions. It wasn't hard to figure out."

"Regardless, he was lucky."

"Unlike the people in the truck," Bella said grimly.

AFTER GRAHAM LEFT the accident scene, Bella continued to help sort people out, sending them to either the Carriage House or the park. She encouraged the bystanders to go home but some of them simply wouldn't leave. The people in the park were mostly from the bus and generally unhurt. A number of them were asking what they were supposed to do now that the bus was out of commission. Then Bella spied an older lady sitting by herself on one of the park benches. The lady held a hand to her cheek and had a vacant stare on her face.

"Ma'am? I'm Bella Benson. Can I help you?" As Bella drew near, she realized the lady was holding a tissue to her cheek.

The blank expression cleared and she smiled tremulously at Bella. "No, dear. Thank you. You're sweet to ask. I'm Patsy Sorenson."

"I take it you were on the tour bus."

"Yes. Is everyone all right?"

"Honestly, I don't know. I do know some people have been taken to the hospital. Are you badly hurt, Mrs. Sorenson?"

She lowered her hand to show a deep cut on her cheek, bleeding freely. "I don't think so. Just this cut. And please call me Patsy. Would you like to sit down?"

"That cut looks pretty deep. Shouldn't you go to the

hospital to see if you need stitches?"

"Oh, that's a lot of bother for nothing. I'm fine. I just need my cheek to quit bleeding. And to find a way to get my car," she added. "It's over in Fredericksburg where the tour started."

Bella wondered how they planned to get all the people back to Fredericksburg, but right now, she was concerned with one person. "Why don't I take you to the hospital? I'm sure there will be something set up for the less serious injuries. And after they fix you up, I'll take you to your car."

"Oh, honey, I can't ask you to do that."

"It's no trouble at all, Patsy. I'll go get my car and come back to pick you up. It's a silver Camry."

Patsy blinked back tears. "That's the kindest thing any-one has done for me in ages."

"I'm happy to help. I'll be back in a few minutes."

And that's how Bella wound up at Jameson, the name the locals gave to the hospital, waiting while Patsy was taken care of. The older lady had looked so lost and lonely that Bella's heart went out to her. And once Patsy confessed she had gone on the tour alone, Bella was doubly determined to help her.

"Bella?"

She looked up to see Graham. He'd changed into his scrubs and had his lab coat on and looked very professional and not a little imposing. But his eyes looked tired and she felt a sudden rush of sympathy for him and all the medical personnel who would be working double shifts until things settled down.

"Hi. You look beat. Are you going to get to go home soon?"

He shook his head. "No. We've had several cases of chest pain, but luckily everyone but the man you, me, and Sean worked on were false alarms. But I'm sticking around to make sure my patient is recovering well."

"That's good then. Were there any more fatalities than the two your brother told us about?" She'd seen the vehicle upside down, crushed and charred, sitting up against the statue of old Asa Fuhrmann in front of the library. She was only surprised that even one of the people in that mess had survived.

"Just the two at the scene. So far," he added wearily. "Other than August Wolf's vintner and vineyard manager, who were inside the building, and the burn victim from the truck, most of the injuries were minor. Cuts, bruises, a couple of broken bones and Everett Ramsey gave everyone a scare. At first, we thought he'd been hit by the bus, but he'd fallen trying to get out of the way. Thank God he didn't break a hip, although I'm not sure how he avoided it."

"What a horrible way to end Mrs. H's birthday party. She's all right, isn't she?" It suddenly occurred to Bella that she hadn't heard anything about the honoree.

"She's not at the hospital and I guarantee you she would be if something was wrong with her. I'm sure someone at the party took her home."

"Well, at least that's good." She saw Patsy come out of the double doors that opened into the waiting room and motioned to her when she saw her looking around. Patsy's eyes widened and she shook her head, taking a seat and clearly waiting for Bella.

"What's wrong?" Graham asked.

"Oh, I brought a lady here who was on the bus and she had a gash that needed stitches. She probably doesn't want to interfere in our conversation. I was waiting until she was finished here to take her to her car over in Fredericksburg."

"Over and above the call of duty," Graham said with a smile.

"Don't be silly," she said, though the way he was looking at her made her heart beat a bit faster. "I only did what anyone would have done seeing her sitting there all alone."

"No. Not everyone. In fact, most people wouldn't have bothered." He reached out and tweaked a curl. "You did what a very observant and thoughtful person would do. You're kind as well as beautiful."

Their gazes met and Bella sucked in a breath at the intensity of his gaze. He'd doubtlessly known other women far more beautiful than she was, but the way he said it, in that deep, sonorous voice, made her believe she was the only one. *Damn, he really is dangerous.*

Chapter Three

O N THE TENTH of every month, the McBrides held family poker night at the ranch. The only excuses for not attending were work, illness, being out of town, or death, and God help you if you lied about work or being sick and were found out. Graham didn't mind since he liked his family. Usually. But like all families, sometimes they got on each other's nerves.

Graham's mom, Rita, would make her specialty, a big pot of fire-engine hot chili and corn bread, and everyone else was required to bring something to eat or drink, even if it was only a bag of corn chips or a six-pack of beer. Everyone except for Jessie, who lived at the ranch and helped set up.

Graham ran into Turner at work a couple of days after the tour bus accident.

"Are you going to the ranch tonight?" Turner asked him. Turner was the sibling nearest to Graham in age, and the one he was closest to.

"Tonight? Crap, it's the tenth, isn't it? Seems like we just had poker night."

"We did. Last month."

"I'll be there but I'll be damned if I'm going to muck out

her stalls if Jessie wins."

"Good luck with that. *When* Jessie wins," Turner added.

Graham sighed. "Yeah." Unfortunately, their sister Jessie usually won at their monthly poker night. And when she did, she won labor, as well as money. Not much money since they played for low stakes, per Rita's command. But when Jessie won, the losers were also required to help with her horses, which often meant mucking out stalls. Or something even worse. "We should never have taught her how to play poker."

"Blame Spencer. He's the one who lobbied for it."

"Hell, she was eight years old. Who figured she'd become a card shark?"

"I don't think Mom was surprised," Turner said.

"That's because Mom is almost as good as Jessie."

"You know, it seems unfair that the two women in the family are the best poker players."

"Damn straight," Graham said. "Speaking of our parents, aren't Mom and Dad still out of town?" The elder McBrides had been called away on a family emergency, and so were unable to attend Minna Herdmann's birthday party. Otherwise they'd never have missed it. Doc had been Minna's GP for years and she still hadn't forgiven him for retiring.

Jessie, though the youngest and a girl, ruled the family in everything concerning the ranch. And in some other things as well. Poker night was one of them.

Graham enjoyed it. He didn't like losing, of course. But he liked being with his family.

Most of the time.

Later that evening Graham met his brothers and sister at the ranch. Spencer was technically off, and hoping he wouldn't get called in. As everyone knew and even she admitted, Jessie couldn't cook worth a damn, so luckily their longtime housekeeper, Ruby, made one of her specialties—chicken fried steak, cream gravy, and garlic mashed potatoes.

"Ruby, you're a treasure," Spencer said, taking a bite of his dinner.

"This is great," Graham said. "What would we do without you?"

"Get food poisoning if Jessie cooked," Turner said. "But I agree. Nobody makes chicken fried steak like you do, Ruby."

"Hey, I'm not that bad," Jessie said.

They all looked at her in varying degrees of disbelief.

"Oh, sweetie, yes you are," Ruby said, drawing a laugh from all of them.

After dinner, they got down to business.

Several games in, Graham decided tonight might be a good one after all. For a change, he had been winning.

"Fold, damn it," Turner said tossing down his cards. "Damn, I hate it when the cards suck."

"Are you sure it's the cards?" Jessie asked.

"She's got you there, Turner."

"Funny, funny," Turner said. "Anybody want a beer?"

"I'll take one," Graham said.

"So, Graham, I hear you're robbing the cradle," Spencer said. Having folded early on, he was thumbing through one of Jessie's *Horse and Rider* magazines.

"You heard wrong." Graham glared at his youngest brother.

"Don't look at me. It's all over town."

Of course it was. This was Last Stand, after all. Where everyone knew everyone else's business.

"What's all over town?" Jessie asked.

"Graham's been hitting on Bella Benson," Turner told her. "You know, the cute blonde who owns the beauty shop on Main."

"I'm not hitting on her. I asked her out." Which wasn't at all the same thing.

"I don't know her well but I like Bella," Jessie said. "What's wrong with Graham asking her out?"

"Nothing," Spencer said and added, "Except he's fifteen or twenty years older than she is."

"Bullshit," Graham said. "She's twenty-five. And I'm still in my thirties."

"Not for much longer," Turner said.

Graham shot him the bird. "For God's sake, it's a simple date. I'm not asking her to marry me."

"Touchy, touchy," Spencer said.

"Bite me." There were two queens and a jack, a seven of diamonds and a two of spades on the table. And he was sitting with two jacks in his hand. Not very much could beat a full house of jacks and queens. "I'm all in," he said to Jessie and pushed his chips to the center. "Call."

"All in," she said and pushed all her chips to the middle. "Cards on the table," she told him.

His brothers had perked up with the showdown. With a

smile, Graham laid his cards on the table. "Full house," he said unnecessarily.

"Nice hand," Jessie said. He reached for the chips and she said, "Not so fast, Bro." She laid out her hand. "Four queens."

"Shit."

Turner and Spencer hooted and hollered. "Damn, Jessie, you are so lucky," Turner said.

Jessie laughed and gathered the chips. "It's all that clean living I do. Graham, how about mucking out stalls for me? On your next day off."

Graham gritted his teeth. "You know damn well you have help whose job it is to muck out the stalls."

"But they don't do nearly as good a job as you do."

"Oh, bullshit. You just like to see me up to my waist in horse shit."

"Well, there is that," she said, dealing another hand. "So when did you get interested in Bella? I didn't think you even knew each other."

"The matchmaker introduced them at Mrs. H's party," Spencer said before Graham could speak. "Two," he said, laying down two cards.

"How do you know?" Graham asked. "You weren't even there."

"Turner told me."

"Damn, can't you two mind your own business?"

"No," Spencer said. "It's more fun to mind yours. For one thing, Turner has no business talking about anything other than medicine."

"You're one to talk, changeling."

Jessie groaned. "Now you've done it." Spencer, the only blond one in the family, had endured a lot of teasing over the years because he didn't look like the rest of them.

"You're just jealous of my good looks," Spencer told Turner. "And youth."

Turner made a gagging sound while the rest of them laughed.

"You didn't have to ask her out, you know," his sister said. "Why do you let Clara do that to you?"

"Have you ever seen Clara's disappointed face?"

"Well, no, but—"

"Then don't ask stupid questions. Besides, I like Bella. She's different."

"Different how?"

"I think it's her hair."

"Her hair?" Turner asked. "What about her hair?"

"It was rainbow colored."

All three of his siblings stared at him.

"That so totally doesn't sound like someone you'd date," Jessie said.

Graham shrugged. "I've seen people with odd-colored hair before and never thought much about it. But Bella's was really pretty."

"You're scaring me, Bro," Turner said. "This sounds serious."

"How can it be serious? We just met."

"Yeah but hearing you fixate about her hair..."

"I'm not fixated. I just liked it. And I liked her. She's

different," he repeated.

Spencer shook his head. He and Turner started talking about basketball, having decided, apparently, to forget about Graham's love life.

"Where are you taking her?" Jessie asked him.

"I'm meeting her at the festival."

Jessie stared at him. "Since when do you go to the Bluebonnet Festival?"

"When I'm not working."

"Turner told me you always volunteer to be on call so you don't have to go."

Graham shot his brother a dirty look but since Turner and Spencer were still talking he didn't even notice. "I volunteer so the people with kids can go." At least, that's what he always told himself. Honestly, it was because every time he attended an event like that, he saw so many people that he knew, or worse, should have known and didn't, that he was exhausted by the end of it. Although, he'd made an exception for Minna's party and was glad he had. Usually, though, he found working more satisfying than dealing with a crowd of people.

"I'm riding in the parade," Jessie said. "Are you coming to that?"

He hadn't planned on it, but Jessie looked so hopeful that he realized belatedly that he must have hurt her feelings by not going. She rode in it every year without fail. "Absolutely," he told her. "Which one of the horses are you riding?"

"Maple," she said. "She likes to show off."

Graham smiled. "She's a pretty horse." Maple had gotten her name because she was the color of maple syrup and was just as sweet.

"What about you two?" he asked his brothers. If he had to go so should they.

"I'm driving the fire engine in the parade," Spencer said.

"I'm helping with the chamber of commerce float," Turner said.

"How'd you get tapped for that?"

"Charlie volunteered me," Turner said with a sigh. Charlotte "Charlie" Stockton owned Char-Pie, the pie shop on Main Street. She and Turner had known each other for a long time and she liked to volunteer him for different civic events and projects. Graham couldn't figure out how she got him to agree but although he grumbled, Turner always did what she signed him up for.

"How is Charlie?" Spencer asked. "Is she dating Wallace?"

Turner frowned. "Yeah. I warned her about him but she told me to butt out."

Jessie laughed. "What's wrong, are you jealous?"

"No. I just happen to know he's a player and that's the last thing Charlie needs."

"I don't blame her for ignoring you. Rick Wallace is hot."

"Damn, Jessie. I'd better not hear about you dating him."

"Too late," Jessie said cheerfully. "I already have."

"What?" Rick Wallace was an ER doc at the hospital,

and the last person Graham wanted his little sister dating. He wasn't a bad guy, but as Turner said, he was definitely a player. "When was this?"

"A while ago. Don't get your shorts in a twist. Nothing came of it. But I can definitely see why Charlie would date him."

"He's a total player," Turner insisted again. "You'd think she'd have more sense."

Jessie laughed. "When did you get so straitlaced? Maybe she just wants to have a little fun. It's not like any of you have settled down. In fact, from what I hear, all of you are players too."

"No, we're not," they said in unison.

"Oh, really? When's the last time any of you had a serious girlfriend?"

"Been there, done that, not doing it again," Graham said. "I have an ex-wife, remember?"

"How many years ago was that? Ten or more, wasn't it?"

"So?"

"She's got you there, Bro," Turner said. "Are you going to let one bad experience ruin you for all women?"

"Since when is this 'gang up on Graham' night?"

"Better you than us," Spencer said.

"Maybe I should warn Bella," Jessie said. "After all—"

"You do and I'll tell Mom you were the one who broke her favorite lamp playing football in the house."

"You wouldn't. Besides, that was ages ago."

"It was last Christmas and she's still pissed about it."

"Spoilsport. You know I wouldn't say anything bad

about you to Bella. For one thing, it's high time you got over Cruella doing you wrong and realized not all women are like her."

Ever since they'd divorced, Jessie never referred to Cynthia as anything other than *Cruella*. "I don't think all women are like her," Graham protested. Only some of them. When he and Cynthia were first married, he'd been in medical school and she'd been in law school. She'd often talked about her ambition to join a prestigious law firm. But once married, she'd quickly changed her mind. She dropped out before finishing and after that, their marriage hadn't been the same. After medical school, Graham's internship and residency became even more time-consuming and demanding and they hardly saw each other. So she'd gotten a job. And had an affair with her boss.

End of marriage.

"Oh, really?" Jessie said. "Prove it."

"Right. I'm not getting married just to prove a point."

"I'm not telling you to get married. But date someone longer than a couple of months."

Since he hadn't even had his first date with Bella, he couldn't say that would happen. But if he was honest, Jessie was right. He hadn't dated a woman seriously since his divorce.

BELLA HAD BEEN half afraid Graham would call off their date, but he didn't. In fact, he'd called her the day after the party to confirm. She chose her outfit for the festival carefully. Since she'd be wearing it all day and night, it had to be comfortable. And of course, she had to look fabulous in it— or if not fabulous, at least good—since she was meeting Graham that afternoon. She didn't want to be too casual. She needed to look professionally casual since she'd basically be an advertisement for her salon.

She wound up wearing a black sundress with spaghetti straps. Small orangey-red chrysanthemums were sprinkled randomly over the dress, but there was a band of evenly spaced flowers circling the hem. She'd looked longingly at a pair of reddish wedges with a four-inch heel, but she couldn't do that to her feet since she'd be on them for hours. Instead she chose flat dark orange strappy sandals that laced partway up her legs.

And she streaked her hair with reddish orange—the same color as the flowers on her dress. Just a few streaks for emphasis, not all over. A few bangle bracelets and red and orange dangly beaded earrings completed her outfit.

Bella's booth was very busy most of the day. Kids and parents alike wanted to try something different. The chalk she used washed out after one or two shampoos, which calmed the nerves of some of the moms. She had help so was able to take a break, but by three o'clock she'd cut her helpers loose…then wished she hadn't, since she got even busier. She'd just finished streaking a girl's hair purple when she heard Graham's voice. "Looks like you've had a busy day."

Bella looked up and smiled at him. "I have. Does this

mean it's four? I haven't even had time to blink since I let everyone go."

"It's a little before. I've seen lots of colored hair in the crowd."

"I can't take credit for all of it, but people like it. Want me to give you a streak?" She paused and added, "How about orange?"

"You want to put an orange streak in my hair?"

"Bright orange. Sure. It will be fun." He looked...not quite appalled.

"I'll have to pass on that. I don't think my patients would like their doctor to have unnaturally colored hair."

"Well that's stuffy. Besides it washes out."

"Sorry. No can do." But he smiled when he said it.

"I was teasing, you know." She hadn't expected him to agree but she didn't think it hurt to try.

"Were you?"

"Well, mostly."

He laughed. "I think I'll leave the hair colors to you." He reached out and touched her hair. "It suits you."

There wasn't a reason in the world why Graham touching her hair and smiling at her should make her go all fluttery. Nevertheless, it did. She'd liked him from afar but in person he was even more appealing.

Quit staring at the man like a fool.

But he's so pretty.

Not pretty. He's hot.

Whatever. He's worth staring at.

"Bella? Is something wrong?"

"No. Sorry, I was thinking about…cleaning up here."
Oh, that's brilliant, Bella.

"Can I help you with that?"

"Sure. I've got to pack this stuff up and drop it off at the shop. Would you mind carrying the card table?"

"Not a bit. I'll carry the chair too."

"My hero."

"Wow, if that's all I have to do to be a hero, what will you say when I spring for barbecue?"

She pretended to think as she gathered up the temporary colors. "Be still my heart?"

"Even better."

Bella laughed and finished putting her colors and instruments in the bag she'd brought for that purpose. "Have you been at the festival all day?"

"Not all day. I came this morning to see Jessie and the parade but after that I went home and came back about half an hour ago. The festival has grown a lot since I last came to one."

"When was that?"

"Honestly, I can't remember. Several years ago, at least."

On the way to Bella's shop, she began to get an inkling of why Graham might shy away from things like the festival. They couldn't go three feet before someone he knew saw him and wanted to talk. After about the fifth person stopped them she said something about it. "Are you always so popular?" It wasn't only women who stopped him, either. He seemed to know everyone in town. But then, he was home grown, so she shouldn't be surprised.

"I know a lot of people here. But if you think this is bad, you should go to the grocery store with my father. It takes three times as long to make it through the store than if you're alone."

"He's retired now, isn't he?"

"He is. But that doesn't stop anyone from telling him their medical issues."

Bella laughed. "I can imagine them stopping him in the aisle to talk about their ailments. He was a general practitioner, right? He probably knows a ton of people around here."

"Yeah, and delivered most of the people around my age and younger, and then he started on their kids' kids."

"So he delivered two generations of kids?"

Graham nodded. "And a few of the third generation."

"Wow. So did he primarily practice OB-GYN?"

"No, when he started, he did it all. Surgery, obstetrics, orthopedist, internist. But as the hospital grew and more specialists came, he gradually stopped practicing so many of the specialties."

Bella stumbled but before she could fall, Graham had dropped the chair and reached out to steady her. She found herself smack up against his side, gazing into his eyes. His arm tightened around her and his gaze dropped to focus on her mouth. For a moment, she thought he was going to kiss her but he didn't. Instead saying, "Steady there."

"Thanks. I wasn't paying attention." He didn't need to know she was a certified klutz. Not yet, anyway.

He let go of her. "The ground is uneven here."

She appreciated him making the excuse, even though they both knew the ground was damn near as smooth as a baby's bottom. "Did you always want to be a doctor?"

"Since high school, yes. When I was little I wanted to be a fireman. But I left that to my brother Spencer."

That's right. His brother Spencer was a paramedic and firefighter. She'd met him at the scene of the accident. "Did you want to be a doctor since your dad was one?"

"Partly. It's a tradition in our family. But—" He hesitated, then said, "This is going to sound corny but I wanted to help people."

"I don't think that's corny at all. I think it's admirable. It must be very satisfying."

"It can be. When everything goes well."

When they reached her shop, she unlocked the door and let Graham in. After locking up behind him, she explained, "I can't compete with your father or you, but people have been known to think I'm open if the door is unlocked. And some of them think I must have forgotten to change the sign if they see me in here."

"And you have a hard time turning them down."

"How do you know that?"

"Just a guess."

"Unfortunately, you're right. But not today."

"Your shop is bigger than I expected," he said, looking around.

"It used to be an antique store, but that was a long time ago."

"You've done a nice job with it."

"Thanks. I'm pretty proud of it." She showed him where to put the card table and chairs, put up her own things and was ready to go. "What do you want to do first?"

"Honestly?"

"Of course."

He smiled, slow and sexy as sin. Then he cupped her face in his hands and kissed her.

Chapter Four

S HE TASTED SWEET with a hint of spice. Her lips were soft and giving, opening slowly when he traced them with his tongue. Tempted to pull her close and deepen the kiss, he kept his hands on her face. He didn't want to overwhelm her. His reward was her response, her tongue doing a slow dance with his, her mouth opening to let him explore.

Regretfully, he ended the kiss, but he kept his hands where they were and smiled at her. "I've wanted to kiss you since about thirty seconds after we were introduced." He let go of her but stayed where he was.

She laughed. "I'd have paid to see the expression on Clara's face if you had."

"Yes, me too. But as you can see, I restrained myself."

"Do you often want to kiss women you've just met?"

"No. You're the first." He realized with a shock that it was true. He'd dated a lot of women, but he hadn't felt an immediate desire to kiss them. Not even his ex-wife, and she'd bowled him over at first.

"You're very good at bullshit. I almost believe you."

"Believe it. Although, I am good at bullshitting," he added modestly, as they left the shop.

The festival was a huge draw for a lot of arts and crafts, from quilts to artwork, to jewelry, to stained glass and everything in between. There was every kind of food—corn dogs, funnel cakes and cotton candy to barbecue and fried turkey legs and other food from the local restaurants and farmers. There were local craft beers and a wine walk hosted by the area wineries. He noticed August Wolf had a tent going for his wine, and was a little surprised since his tasting shop had been messed up so badly from the tour bus crashing into it.

They started to walk by a funnel cake stand and Bella stopped dead. "Bella?"

She inhaled. "That smell is delicious. I'm just thinking about the last time I had funnel cake and how good it was."

Obviously, she wanted a funnel cake. Graham bought one and gave it to her.

"Share it with me," she said.

"I haven't had funnel cake since I was a kid."

"All the more reason to have some now."

They found an unoccupied table and sat down. Fried dough with cinnamon and powdered sugar. Graham admitted it looked good, and tasted even better. "I'm afraid to touch anything," Graham said, holding up his sticky hands after they finished.

"Me too," Bella said, and pulled a couple of packets out of her purse, handing him a wet wipe. "I knew I wasn't going to resist funnel cake."

"Smart woman."

They cleaned up and she asked, "Did I get it all?"

"Not quite." He wiped the corner of her mouth with his thumb and licked it. "Powdered sugar. Sweet," he said, thinking about the kiss they'd shared earlier. Her eyes darkened and he wondered if she was thinking about it too.

"Have you always lived in Last Stand?" she asked him.

Apparently she wasn't.

"I know your family has a ranch," Bella continued.

"Yes, except for school and my training. I lived here until I went to college at UT Austin, then medical school at Southwestern in Dallas. So you and I have lived some of the same places. But I did my internship and residency at Duke."

"Which is where?"

"North Carolina."

"Did you like it there?"

"It was all right. I worked a lot." And when he hadn't been working, which wasn't often, he'd been trying, unsuccessfully, to fix his failing marriage. But that wasn't a subject he liked to discuss. Not with anyone, much less a woman he was interested in.

Surprisingly, she didn't push for more. Instead she spotted a dart game where the object was to burst balloons. They both played. Bella came away with a stuffed animal. Graham won a plastic duck. "Where'd you learn to play darts?"

"I'm self-taught. I have a dart board at home."

"You're very good."

"Thanks. I'm even better with an actual dart board."

"A woman of many talents."

Bella laughed.

"See anything else you want to try?" Graham asked her.

"Shoot out the star," she replied promptly.

That's where Graham discovered Bella was quite competitive. They both took a turn at shooting and while hers was very good, Graham's was better, which didn't please her at all. "Remember, I grew up on a ranch, Bella. We learned to shoot when we were little. Lots of varmints on a ranch."

"Still, I've been going to Lock and Load regularly for a while now. I should be better. Clearly, I need more practice."

He knew that Lock and Load was the shooting range on the outskirts of town. "I've never been there. If we want to shoot, we take some bottles out. Or set up some stands with paper targets."

"Do you do that a lot?"

"Not so much anymore. We used to have regular competitions with all of us kids."

"That sounds like fun."

"It was. Until Jessie started beating the pants off of all of us."

"Did it bother you and your brothers to be beaten by a girl?"

Graham laughed. "Not any more than it did to be beaten by any one of us. Our mother is the best shot of all of us. She's scarily good."

"What about your dad? Does he shoot?"

"Sometimes. Not very often."

"I can't imagine what it's like having a big family."

"You don't have any siblings?"

She shook her head. "No. I was an only child."

He waited but she didn't say any more. "You said you'd

been on your own since you were seventeen."

"Yes. My mother died when I was sixteen. Cancer. My father died about a year later. He had a heart attack."

"I'm sorry. It must have been rough losing them when you were so young."

"It was. They were good parents. My dad was never the same after my mom died. I wonder if he had a premonition about his own death. He pushed me pretty hard to figure out what I wanted to do as a career. But he died before I figured it out."

"Did you go into the system?"

"No. I lived with a friend until I turned eighteen and graduated high school. It was only for a few months. My parents left me some money. Not enough for college, but I probably wouldn't have gone anyway. My dad wanted me to go, but school was never my thing." She looked at him. "I guess that sounds odd to you. Not wanting to go to college."

"Not odd. Just different from my experience."

"You had a zillion years of schooling, didn't you?"

Graham laughed. "Not quite a zillion. But yes, I had quite a bit."

"Well, I took the money and went to cosmetology school. I'd always been good with hair, and I liked messing with it, so that seemed like a no-brainer. And that's the story of my life. More or less. Your turn."

"We already talked about me."

"We talked about your education and a tiny bit about your family. We haven't talked about whether you like what you do or what your hobbies are or if you have any pets."

"You haven't answered those questions either," Graham said.

"I will if you will."

"Deal. You first."

"All right. I love what I do. I have a cat named Abby. She adopted me not long after I came to town. I'd never had a pet before. Mom was allergic to most animals. Abby usually comes to the shop with me." She put a finger to her cheek. "Let's see, what else? Oh, my hobbies are reading and painting."

"So you're an artist?"

"No, I just like to paint. I suck at it, but I like to experiment with colors."

"Have you ever been married?"

"No. Not engaged either."

Which wasn't a surprise, considering her age. But it made him remember their age difference.

"I was serious about a guy, but it didn't work out."

"I'm sorry."

"Don't be. He was a jerk. Okay, Graham, your turn."

He'd never had a conversation with a woman he was interested in that was quite like this one. "I love what I do. Some people think I'm a workaholic but I'm not. I'm a surgeon. We work a lot. It's what we do. Which is why I don't have a pet. Also why I'm divorced, come to think of it. If I need an animal fix, I can go to the ranch where there's all kinds of critters. I play a little poker and racquetball whenever I get the chance. And finally, it's not a hobby but I help Jessie with the horses sometimes."

"If it isn't a hobby, what is it?"

"Generally payment for losing to her at poker."

Bella laughed. "That's great."

"For Jessie, sure." One of the bands started playing a rock tune. They sat and listened to them for a bit and when Graham noticed Bella tapping her foot to the music he said, "Do you want to dance?"

"Oh, no. That's okay. I'm fine just listening."

"You're tapping your foot. Are you sure you don't want to dance?"

She sighed. "I might as well tell you now. I can't dance."

"You mean you don't like to dance?"

"No, I love to dance. But I can't. Not in public. I'm awful at it."

"I have a hard time believing that." Apart from stumbling a couple of times, Bella was very graceful.

"Believe it. I never learned and whenever I tried, it was a disaster. So I just don't even try anymore."

"Do you want to learn how?"

"I told you, I'm hopeless."

"That's not an answer." He got up and held out a hand. "Come on."

"Where to?"

"Where's your sense of adventure?"

"I'm not making a fool of myself in public."

"Duly noted." He continued to hold out his hand and she reluctantly put hers in his. Her hand was small, like the rest of her, but her grip was firm. Graham led her around behind one of the tents a short way away from the music. "Is this private enough?"

Bella looked around. "I guess."

He put one arm around her waist and took her hand with the other. "Relax."

"I can't."

"Sure you can."

Apparently, she couldn't. She was clearly nervous and kept stepping on his boots. Once she managed to make him step on her foot. She yelped, which made him feel like a jerk, even though it hadn't really been his fault.

"Damn, I'm sorry," Graham said.

"I told you I was hopeless."

"No, you're not." He let go of her and sat on the ground.

"What are you doing?"

"What does it look like?" He yanked off a boot and started on the other.

"Why are you taking off your boots?"

"Take off your shoes."

"Why?"

"Stop arguing, Bella. Just do it."

She grumbled but she did it. Soon they were both barefoot. He put his arms around her again and said, "Step on my feet."

"That's silly."

"Do you want to learn to dance or not?"

She stepped on his feet and he started moving.

"I feel stupid," she said. "I don't like feeling stupid."

"No one does. But there's no reason to feel stupid. Lots of people can't dance. It's not a big deal."

"Then why are you trying to teach me?"

"Because you were sitting there listening to the music and tapping your foot and you looked wistful."

"I did not."

"Yeah, you did." He smiled down at her. "Guess what?"

"What?"

"You're dancing."

She looked surprised and then she smiled. Bella had a very infectious smile. "Oh, my God. You're right. I'm—"

"Dancing. Now try it on your own."

Gingerly, she stepped off of his feet. He continued to hold her and moved to the music. Her brow furrowed and she bit her lip in concentration, staring at her feet. "Hey, I'm up here," Graham said.

She raised her gaze to look at him. "I'm concentrating."

"Yes, I can see that. Relax. Just feel the rhythm."

"How am I supposed to relax? If I don't concentrate—"

"You dance perfectly well."

Bella looked startled. "I'm dancing."

"Yep."

"On my own. And not getting my feet tangled up." She jammed her foot beneath his. "Oops. Spoke too soon." Her eyes sparkled and she laughed heartily. "Damn, I almost had it."

"You are so dang cute when you laugh like that."

She laughed again. "Cute?"

"Cute," he affirmed and kissed her.

IT WAS EVEN better than the first kiss, Bella thought. Still not pushy, but more intense. But while he had initiated the kiss, he let her set the pace. She wrapped her arms around his neck and deepened the kiss. She hadn't kissed anyone in a long time, except for her friend Rex, and she didn't count him. Those had been platonic, at least on her part. This was anything but.

Maybe it was just the romance of it. The warm night, soft music, the feeling that they were alone in the world. Being held in his arms while he kissed her and feeling desire spreading through her blood. A part of her counseled caution, but the other part, the impulsive side of her, wanted to just go for it.

He ended it before she was ready. Left her wanting more. Which he undoubtedly knew.

"Notice anything?" he asked her.

"Uh, the rumors are true?"

"What rumors?"

"Some of your dates have been in my shop and they all say one thing."

"Do I want to know what?"

"They say you're a good kisser. Very good and very smooth."

"I guess that's better than the alternative. But I was talking about something else. You've been dancing for the last several minutes and haven't stomped on my foot or managed to make me stomp on yours."

He was right. She hadn't screwed up in at least ten minutes. "I must have had a good teacher."

"Thank you, ma'am."

"No one else has ever tried to teach me to dance. They pretty much just disappeared when I said I didn't know how. Thank you."

"My pleasure."

They danced until the band took a break. During the break they wandered around the festival, holding hands and looking at all the things for sale. Graham insisted on buying anything Bella said she liked. After he bought her a wood carving of a cat and a painting of the bluebonnet trail, she kept her mouth shut. She wondered what he'd do if she picked something really expensive but she wasn't about to test him. He'd probably buy it.

Another band took the first one's place and Graham convinced her to brave the dance area. Since there were a ton of people dancing and jostling each other, she didn't feel as self-conscious as she would have before. Besides, she was getting better at it and she had to admit she liked being so close to him. She liked it a lot.

After they tired of dancing, they wandered around again. A couple of microbreweries had set up tents, which they hit up. "There's something about good, cold beer that just hits the spot," Bella said, sipping one. "Much more so to me than wine. But then, I've never had good wine, so what do I know?"

"I've had good wine before and while I like it, I still like beer better."

See, you do have something in common.

Eventually the festival wound down. The booths closed,

the bands quit playing, tents came down and only a few people remained. Graham walked with her to her car, which was parked behind her shop.

"I had fun," she said.

"So did I."

"You sound surprised."

"I am, a little. I haven't been to the Bluebonnet Festival in years, so I wasn't sure what to expect. But it was fun." He stepped closer, and took her in his arms. "Because of you." He leaned down and kissed her.

His lips pressed against hers; his tongue traced the seam of her lips. She opened her mouth and let him inside, her tongue tangling with his. He took his time, as if he was savoring the kiss, and while he held her close, his hands stayed on her back and didn't wander further south.

Oh, my God, I'm tingling. From a kiss?

He let her go and smiled at her. "I'll call you."

"Bye."

I'll call you. What every man said at the end of a date. At least half the time they didn't mean it. Did Graham?

Chapter Five

B Y THE TIME Bella got to the shop to open on Tuesday morning, her friend, Delilah Corbyn, was standing at the front door waiting impatiently to get in. "I'm sorry I'm late, Delilah," she said a little breathlessly. Balancing her cat under one arm, she opened the door. "Come on in."

"You're never late. Why are you late?" Delilah, a slim, petite blonde, looked like an innocent angel but Bella was well aware her friend could be hell on wheels when she needed to be. Since Delilah owned and was the chef at the Dragonfly Farm to Table restaurant out on Hickory Creek, Bella knew she often needed to be decisive. If nothing else, to keep her employees in line. But she was a fair boss and paid well, so there were always people wanting to work there. And Delilah's talent as a chef was undeniable.

"I stayed up late and overslept. Thank goodness Abby woke me, but she's been annoyed with me ever since." They both glanced at the cat, who took time from cleaning her paws in the front window to glare at Bella. "I fed her dry kibble."

"Shame on you! I don't blame her a bit."

"She's such a princess."

"And whose fault is that?"

"Good point."

Delilah sat in Bella's chair. The other stylists, the nail technician, and the esthetician began to trickle in. Bella greeted everyone and turned back to her friend.

"What are we doing today? You could use a trim."

"Oh, definitely. But the main reason I came was because I loved the way you did your hair at Mrs. Herdmann's party and I've been dying to try it out. Not my whole head like yours, but I want the ends dipped in rainbow colors. Can you do it?"

"Sure. How long do you want the color to stay?"

"Since I've never done it before can you do something that will wash out easily?"

"Yes. Now, let's pick some colors. The lighter ones—like pastels—will wash out more easily," she cautioned. Since Delilah's hair was dark blonde, Bella knew it would hold color longer than darker hair. She washed, trimmed and dried Delilah's hair while trying to keep track of all the tangents her friend went off on. Then she began putting on pastel blue.

"And now, what about you?" Delilah asked. "How was your date with Graham McBride?"

Both Delilah and Joey knew she'd gone out with Graham but she hadn't talked to either of them since.

"The date was great," she said, finishing the blue and starting on the pink.

Delilah clapped her hands. "Details! I need details."

"There aren't a lot. We hung out at the festival. It was

fun."

"That's it? That's all you've got to say?"

Now green. Bella was careful with green, not wanting it to look as if chlorine simply hadn't been washed out. "He bought me a wooden cat and a painting."

Delilah looked at her in the mirror. "A nice painting?"

"Not expensive, if that's what you mean. But I like it."

"And?"

Bella frowned. "He's a better shot than I am. He says it's because he grew up on a ranch." Delilah's shoulders shook. "Stop laughing unless you want green on your nose."

"I'm sorry. But not really. It's funny to hear you say that when I know you've been busting your butt at the gun range in your spare time."

She had no answer to that so she changed the subject. "He taught me to dance."

"What? You don't know how to dance? Why don't I know this? We've been friends since you came to town."

"I *didn't* know how. Now I do. And since I always felt like a loser, it wasn't something I advertised."

"That was nice, but none of that is very exciting. What else?"

"The rumors are true. He's a very good kisser."

"Better," she said with satisfaction. "Did you sleep with him?"

"It was our first date. What do you think?"

"Damn, Bella, you're no fun."

"I've never slept with a guy on the first date. And yes, I know that's old-fashioned, which is weird, coming from me." Tempted was another matter. Since this was Delilah, she decided to come clean. "Besides, it didn't come up."

"Aha. So you would have."

Bella stopped coloring a strand of hair and shrugged. "It's a moot point. But he is pretty tempting," she admitted.

"Are you seeing him again?"

She thought about what Graham had said before he left. "I don't know. He said he'd call me, but he hasn't."

"Uh-oh. That's disappointing."

Again, Bella shrugged. "He *is* a doctor. And it's only been a few days. Maybe he's been busy."

"Too busy to pick up a telephone?"

"You have a point. Damn it." She sighed. "Oh, well, at least I had a good time at the festival. And it's a good thing I didn't sleep with him. Then I'd have been really pissed when he didn't call."

"I'm sorry, Bella. That blows."

"Don't worry, I'll survive. It's not like I've never been disappointed before. Case in point, my unlamented ex-boyfriend, aka the cheater and the jerk." She turned around Delilah's chair so she could look in the mirror. "What do you think?"

Delilah flipped her fingers through her hair, smiling happily. "I love it! Why haven't I done this before? Oh, this is great."

Bella laughed. "That's what we like to hear. A satisfied customer."

THAT'LL TEACH ME to believe that Jessie's bluffing. Graham scooped up another shovelful of horse shit. *She's one of the luckiest people I've ever known.* Mucking out stables. Damn it, he was a doctor. He shouldn't have to deal with horse shit. But he'd let Jessie sucker him so he supposed he deserved what he got.

"Good job," Jessie said, leaning against the open stall door. "I love to see you working hard."

"Ha ha." He leaned on the shovel and glared at her. "You're a sadist."

"Hey, somebody has to do it. Why should Corey have all the fun?"

"Because it's his job." Corey was the teenager who helped out after school and on weekends. Unless something came up, which it often did. But he was a good kid and worked hard when he was there.

Jessie laughed. "Too bad you had to work on Easter. Mom's ham and sweet potatoes were amazing. And Ruby made two of her famous apple pies and left them both for us."

"You don't need to rub it in." Their mom always put on a big family dinner after church on Easter Sunday. Everyone in the family came, unless they were unlucky enough to be working.

"So, I haven't seen you since the festival. Did you have fun?"

"It was all right." Actually, it had been a lot more than all right. Which was the problem. He kept thinking about kissing Bella. Kept thinking he wanted to do it again. And more. A whole lot more.

"When are you and Bella going out again?" Jessie asked.

"I'm not sure that we are."

"Why? I thought you had fun with her?"

"I did." Bella was a lot of fun. Young, pretty, different. And he liked her. Maybe a bit more than he was comfortable with.

Jessie narrowed her eyes at him and set her hands on her hips. "Oh, no you didn't."

"Didn't what?" he asked irritably.

"Don't tell me you did the old, 'I'll call you' and then didn't call her. You don't even need to answer that. I can tell you did from your guilty face."

"I've been busy."

"For almost two weeks? Lame excuse."

True. Very lame. "Since when do you care who I date?"

"I like Bella. I think you two would be good for each other."

"Why?"

"Because you need someone different. And...I don't know, sincere. Real."

"What's that supposed to mean? Are you saying I only date fake women?" It stung that his sister had a point, but not all the women he went out with were that way.

"I'm saying you *mostly* date fake women. Which is deliberate, so you don't really fall for them. I think they date you because you're like a notch on their belt. You know, 'I'm dating Graham McBride. *Dr.* McBride,'" she said in a sticky-sweet voice.

"Thanks a lot." But he couldn't totally deny her take on many of them.

"Not all of them, of course. But you never seem to date any of them for long. You're still hung up on Cruella, aren't you? She is so not worth it."

"I'm not hung up on my ex-wife. I moved on a long time ago." And so had Cynthia. Of course, she'd moved on before they ever divorced.

"Promise?"

He held up a hand. "Swear to God, I'm not hung up on Cynthia. But I'm also not interested in getting serious about anyone."

"So? Maybe Bella's not either. She seems pretty happy with her life." Jessie focused on him, which was never a good thing. "I see what it is. You're scared! Graham McBride, you are scared shitless you'll like her too much."

"That's ridiculous." If it wasn't it should be. "Fine, I'll ask her out again. If nothing else to prove to you that I'm not afraid I'll 'like her too much.' That's one of the dumbest things I've ever heard you say."

"Oh, I seriously doubt that. Are you going to ask her out?"

"I said I would."

"Good," Jessie said, and turned away, but not before he saw a satisfied smile cross her face.

Damn, she'd played him like a fiddle. Again.

But he wasn't alone. She did the same thing to his brothers. She came by it naturally. Their mother had that talent as well.

BELLA HAD GIVEN up hoping that Graham would actually call. Nearly two weeks had gone by since the festival and she hadn't heard a peep from him. So when Rex Rutledge called and asked her to go get some barbecue Saturday night, she said yes. She and Rex were just friends, although she knew he wanted to be more. But she simply didn't feel that way about him. He was a very nice guy…but there was no spark. No sizzle. He'd kissed her a few times and while she didn't have a brother, that's what she imagined it must be like to kiss one. So she'd told him she only wanted to be friends and expected him to hightail it out of her life. But he hadn't.

Sometimes she wondered why.

Ten minutes after she hung up with Rex her phone rang again. She didn't recognize the number and debated not answering, since she'd been getting a lot of robocalls lately. Curiosity got the better of her. "Hello."

"Hi, Bella. It's Graham."

"Graham?" she repeated blankly.

"Graham McBride."

"I know who you are. I was just surprised to hear from you."

"Why? I said I'd call you."

"Almost two weeks ago. I figured you weren't interested." She probably shouldn't have said that since she didn't want him to think she'd moped around wishing he'd call. Which she kind of had.

"You figured wrong. Things have been hectic at work."

She bit her cheek to keep from saying anything bitchy. Like *too hectic to make a phone call*? "Oh," she managed to say.

"I know it's kind of last-minute, but I wondered if you'd let me take you to dinner Saturday night."

Yes, she was petty. It gave her great satisfaction to be able to say, "That sounds nice but I have a date."

"Oh. Well, that's too bad. What about Sunday night? I'm working tomorrow night." He paused and added, "Unless you're involved with someone?"

"If I was I wouldn't have gone out with you at all, much less have kissed you," she said tartly.

"Good to know. I didn't think you would but..."

"But what? Women are like that?"

"Some women are," he said a bit grimly. "I didn't think you were," he repeated.

"Well, I'm not," she said, seriously annoyed now.

Graham laughed. "Wow, I really got off on the wrong foot. I apologize if I sounded judgmental or insulted you. I didn't mean to. And I'm sorry I didn't call you earlier. I should have. Forgive me?"

Damn. What else could she say? "You're forgiven." She left the *this time* implied.

"Thank you. How about we start over? Bella, would you let me take you to dinner on Sunday night?"

"Let me look at my calendar." She picked up a book lying on the table and flipped through pages while holding the phone close to it to make sure he heard. "Yes, I can fit you in."

"Great," he said, with a tremor of what she assumed was laughter in his voice. "Is seven all right?"

"That sounds good."

"I'll see you then."

They hung up and she sat a moment trying to tell herself she shouldn't be so excited. It wasn't as if he'd called her the minute he could after seeing her Friday night. But he had apologized. And regardless, he had called her, so it would be foolish of her to be huffy about the timing.

He'd made her curious, though. When they were telling each other about themselves, he'd told her he was divorced but not why. Which was reasonable, considering that had been their first date. But the comment about some women being 'like that' had her wondering if cheating had been a problem in Graham's marriage. If it was, she thought his wife had cheated on him. Not only because of his comment but also because he didn't seem like the cheating type. Although, she'd been mistaken about that before, she reminded herself sourly. At any rate, if his wife had been unfaithful, then he had a very good reason for not wanting to get too involved.

Fine with her. She'd done that once with a man who hadn't been on the same page. She'd thought he was as serious as she was, only to discover he was cheating on her every time he left town. And he left town a lot. It just proved how gullible she'd been.

Bella didn't intend to be gullible or vulnerable ever again.

Chapter Six

GRAHAM WASN'T SURPRISED to find out Bella was no pushover. She'd called him out on his flimsy excuse, but she'd also accepted his apology. And what the hell had come over him to ask if she was involved with someone? He'd known she wasn't. But for some reason, God knows why, when she'd told him she had a date, he'd felt a flash of…damn, it could only be called jealousy.

Jealous? Him? His cheating ex-wife had cured him of that. When he dated a woman, he let her know before they slept together that he didn't want a serious relationship. And that if they did sleep together, they were exclusive while they dated.

But he'd only had one date with Bella, so she was perfectly within her rights to date anyone she wanted. And to kiss anyone she wanted. And to sleep with—No, he wasn't going there. No, no, no.

By Sunday he'd given up trying to convince himself that he didn't want to take Bella to bed. It had been a futile exercise.

The Peachtree apartments on the corner of Ash Street and Bluebonnet Lane, where Bella lived, was one of the older complexes in Last Stand. The apartments were nothing fancy but they were decent enough. A lot of people who worked at the hospital lived there, including Spencer. They were more affordable than the Millennial Village, which was newer, closer, and where both Graham and Turner lived.

Graham climbed the concrete stairs and knocked on her door. "Coming," he heard her call out. Moments later, she opened it.

"Hi, come on in. I'm almost ready." She left the door open and went to the sofa where a gray-and-black cat lay.

Graham watched her fussing over her cat, Abby. The cat lay stretched out on the sofa, giving him what could only be described as a steely-eyed stare out of cat-green eyes. Bella wore a very simple sleeveless V-neck black dress. It was fitted at her breasts and waist and flared out at her hips. It was blessedly short, ending several inches above her knees, showing off her long, beautiful legs in high-heeled pink sandals with wrap-around straps at her ankles. He usually didn't notice a lot about a woman's clothes, but damn, she looked good.

Her hair was mostly blonde, which he thought might be her natural color, but tonight she'd added two pale pink stripes the exact color of her shoes. Again, the look worked for her.

"You look great," he said.

"Thanks. If you want to sit down a minute, I'm just going to set out some kibble for Abby and then we can leave."

"No rush." He took a seat in one of the chairs beside the couch. Abby looked at him for a moment, then sprang down lightly from the sofa. She meowed, walked to him and began weaving around his legs. She allowed him to pet her in that way cats have. As if they are conferring a great favor on you by allowing you to touch them. By the time Bella returned, Abby was purring up a storm.

"Oh, good. She likes you."

"Is that unusual?"

"No. She likes most people but she doesn't always like my dates."

"I'm glad I passed the test."

"For now," she said. "Don't get too complacent. Cats often change their minds."

He got the feeling Bella was very much "love me, love my cat." Fine with him. He liked cats. And dogs. And horses. And other assorted critters.

"I hope I'm dressed all right. You didn't say where we were going."

"You look perfect. We've got reservations at the Carriage House. I was a little worried that after the accident they might have a drop-off in their business, but I should have known Last Stand residents wouldn't let that happen."

"This is a very supportive community," Bella said. "I was worried about that when I opened the salon, especially because Clippety-Do-Da was such a fixture here. But I swear Dotty Allen was happy because all the younger people had been going to other towns anyway to get their hair done. She told me she was glad I'd keep them in Last Stand and she even put out the word about my shop. The older crowd still go to Clippety-Do-Da. Well, most of them," she added with a twinkle.

"Except Clara Perkins," he said, remembering hers and Bella's matching rainbow hair at Mrs. H's party.

Bella laughed. "Exactly. She has a very adventurous spirit. I'm kinda worried about what she might want me to do to her hair next time." She picked up her purse and with one last head rub for Abby, said, "I'm ready."

"RIGHT THIS WAY," the Carriage House hostess said, picking up two red-leather-covered menus. "How have you been, Graham?"

"Good, thanks, Rhonda. How about you?"

Busy looking around, Bella didn't pay much attention as the two chatted while Rhonda led them to their table.

The main dining room of the Carriage House was a huge room of rustic elegance. A high vaulted ceiling graced with dark wood beams from the original structure overlooked the room. The hardwood floors gleamed with a beautiful polish. Against one wall was a fireplace with a limestone hearth and a carved wooden mantel lined with fresh flowers. Facing the fireplace on the opposite wall was a huge mahogany bar with an enormous mirror behind it. Glass shelves held hard liquor and a few bottles of wine, though most of the wine was in the Carriage House's extensive wine cellar. Bella knew this because one of her friends had a bachelorette party in the wine cellar. It had been a party to remember, even if she had had to drink wine rather than beer.

Barstools with leather seats and wood backs were occupied by people meeting for drinks or waiting for a table. The bartenders were busy, serving people at the bar and readying drinks for the tables.

On the walls were framed pictures of Last Stand through the years, including pictures of the original Carriage House when it functioned as its name implied. Paintings of horses, and horse-drawn carriages by various local artists shared space with the photos.

Along the sides of the big room were cozy booths with dark brown leather backs. Tables covered with snow-white tablecloths, a small bouquet of fresh flowers and crystal votive holders with flickering candles placed in the center were scattered around the room. In the middle of the room were round tables of varying sizes with wood and fabric chairs and similar tablecloths, flowers and votives. Sparkling crystal glasses, black napkins and white china plates completed the picture.

Bella had always loved this room. Although she'd only had dinner at the Carriage House a couple of times, she had met friends for drinks at the bar more often. A curved iron staircase with wooden steps led to a second floor for a more intimate dining experience. Or so she'd heard, having never been up there. She sent Graham a speculative look but he was still speaking to the hostess. Apparently he knew her. Big surprise. She wondered if he'd dated her. Probably, she thought, noticing the assessing glance the woman had given her when they first arrived. Rhonda led them to a small table in the main room, albeit a somewhat secluded corner booth.

Rhonda gave them their menus and said, "Your waiter will be here shortly. Enjoy your dinner, Bella."

"How did she know my name?" Bella asked when she left.

"I just told her."

"Oh. Sorry. I wasn't paying attention."

"What would you like to drink?"

"Could I have a beer?"

He smiled. "Of course. I'll join you."

They both ordered steaks for dinner, since the Carriage House had a reputation for making delicious ones. The menu leaned toward French, with a healthy dose of Texas thrown in. Bella had the au gratin potatoes, one of the specialties of the house, and the house salad. Graham talked her into splitting a French taco—called a *galette*—and invented in Austin by a Frenchman. Instead of the traditional ground beef filling, it consisted of brisket, *queso blanco*, and avocado wrapped in a whole wheat pastry similar to a tortilla. It was also a lot bigger than any taco she'd ever seen.

"Oh, my God. This is amazing," she said after taking a bite.

"It's one of my favorite menu items here."

They talked about work, hers and his. To Bella's surprise they had a few other things in common, more than preferring beer. Such as some days work was really boring and others were so busy they couldn't keep up. And they both loved what they did. When Graham talked about surgery, his eyes lit up and she could hear how much he loved it in his voice. She wondered how he dealt with it when one of his patients didn't make it, but that wasn't anything she'd dream of asking him.

A couple of different women stopped by to say hi to Graham and, apparently, to check her out too. They weren't rude to her. No surprise since they were bound to be too smart to do that in front of Graham. But she got the definite impression they sized her up and found her lacking.

"Did you used to date those women?"

"What women?"

She rolled her eyes.

"Oh, the two who came by and spoke to us?"

She nodded.

Graham shrugged. "Yes. But not in a long time. Why?"

"I got the feeling they were surprised to see you with me." Why, she didn't know, but that was the impression she had.

"I don't know why they would be. You're young, beautiful and smart. What's not to like?"

"About the 'beautiful' comment, thank you but I'm not. I'm curious, though. How do you know I'm smart?" She knew she was bright but men, and some women, often underestimated her. Maybe it was the blonde hair.

"You own your own salon, and in a town where you didn't know a soul, you've made a success of it in less than three years. Clearly, you've got something going on up here," he said, tapping his head.

"Oh." At a loss for how to respond she simply said, "Thank you."

"It's interesting that you blew off the comment about

your looks but are more pleased with the one about your intelligence. Not surprising, but interesting." He picked up her hand lying on the table, turned it over and kissed her wrist, keeping hold of her hand after that. "For the record, I think you're beautiful as well as smart."

She didn't say anything. She was afraid she'd stutter. Graham smiled and kissed her wrist again. Her wrist? Now why in the hell would that make her tingle all over? Yes, it had been a long time since she'd slept with anyone. A very long time. Still, Graham kissing her wrist shouldn't have such an effect on her.

But it did.

Chapter Seven

THEY SAT TALKING after dinner for quite a while, so it was fairly late by the time they left the restaurant. "Do you want to walk down to the saloon?" Graham asked Bella.

"No. I'm so full, I'll pop if I have anything else. Plus if I have more to drink, I'll have a headache in the morning and I hate that."

They walked to his SUV that he'd parked in the restaurant's lot. He started the truck but before he pulled out, he said, "Can I ask you something?"

"Sure."

"At the risk of you ripping my face off, what's the deal with you and the guy you went out with last night? I know you're not in a serious relationship, but you did have a date."

"Rex? He's a friend. Purely platonic."

"Good to know."

"Now I need to ask you a question." He nodded and she said, "In the restaurant, why did you kiss my wrist?"

He turned to her and smiled. "Because what I really wanted to do was this." He cupped her cheek, slid his hand to the back of her head and tugged her forward. Then he kissed her. Her lips parted and he slipped his tongue inside her mouth. Their tongues touched and tangled and the kiss grew hotter. How would it feel to have his hands on her breasts, or better yet, his mouth?

But he didn't take it any further. Instead he ended the kiss, leaving her wanting more.

The drive to her apartment only took a couple of minutes. He parked and walked her to her door, waiting while she unlocked it. Holding the door open, she turned around.

"I'd like to see you again," he said. "Can I call you?"

"That depends."

"On?"

"Are you going to wait two weeks again?"

He laughed ruefully. He'd had a feeling he wouldn't easily live that down. "No. I'm working but I was thinking I'd call you tomorrow."

"In that case, do you want to come in?"

"Yes." He smiled and followed her in.

Bella tossed her keys and purse on a table by the door. She spoke to Abby, who was lying on the chair beside the couch. She looked up, gave Bella a bored glance and went back to sleep.

"Have a seat," she told him. "Would you like a beer? That's all I have. Oh, I've got water."

"No, I'm good." He sat on the couch.

Bella couldn't decide what to do. She hated that her body said one thing but her mind wouldn't quit with the *what ifs*. This had happened before. Most notably with Cody, the cheater. It wasn't just that he'd cheated but he'd lied. He'd told her she was the only one. And by the time she discovered the truth about him, she'd been in love with him for months.

Oh, for God's sake, Graham's not like Cody.

No, I don't think he is. But I need to know that if we have sex, it won't be just a hookup he'll forget the next day.

So what if it is? You're not in love with the man. If it doesn't work out, it can't hurt that badly.

True. But that isn't the only reason I don't do casual sex.

"Deep thoughts?" Graham asked her.

"Oh, sorry. I was…thinking about something."

"Yes, I suspected that," he said with amusement. "Are you going to sit down or are you going to stand there looking like you expect me to pounce on you any moment?"

"Is that how I look?"

"Pretty much. I won't, you know."

She sat beside him. "I didn't think you would." *Bite the bullet, Bella.* She sucked in a breath. "I like you, Graham."

"Good. I like you too. So what's worrying you?"

"Sex."

His eyes widened and he just looked at her for a moment. "Are we going to have sex?"

Oh, God, she was making a mess of this. "I don't know. I mean, it seems like we're heading that way. Aren't we?" Or was she making a total, absolute fool of herself?

A corner of his mouth kicked up. "I hope so."

She let out a sigh of relief. "Thank God. I was hoping I hadn't totally misread the situation."

He was grinning widely now. "You didn't. I want very

HEART OF THE TEXAS DOCTOR

much to make love to you. But—"

"I can't just hook up with a guy." There. She'd said it. "I know a lot of people my age don't think sex is a big deal, but I'm not into the casual thing."

"Okay. So what you're saying is you need a commitment before you have sex?"

"Not exactly." She squirmed uncomfortably. "But I don't want it to be a hookup we just forget about the next day."

"I don't see how anyone could make love to you and forget you the next day. But to be honest, I'm not looking for a long-term relationship."

"The fact that you've dated almost every woman in town kind of clued me in to that," she said dryly.

"I'm not saying it's impossible. But I tried it before and it wound up being a disaster. So if that's what you're looking for, I'm not your guy."

"I've really screwed this up. I'm not looking for a long-term commitment either. But I am looking for an 'as long as it lasts' commitment."

He'd been looking concerned but his brow cleared at that. "I get it now. You want to be exclusive while we're together."

"Yes."

"I'm good with that. I feel that way, too."

Relief swept through her. "You probably think I'm silly to worry about that when we've only had two dates."

"Not silly. Cautious. There's nothing wrong with that."

"I've ruined the mood, haven't I?"

73

Graham laughed and stood up. "That's probably a good thing. Come on." He held out his hand. "Walk me to the door."

"Thank you. For tonight." The jury was still out on whether he'd decide to pursue something with her or simply write her off as way too much trouble.

He put his arms around her and looked down into her eyes. "I'm working all week but I'll be off Saturday and Sunday. Can I take you to dinner Saturday? Maybe take in a movie if you want."

"I'd like that."

Then he kissed her. A sizzling kiss that fired her blood and made her ache, even though he did nothing else. She gave herself up to it, wondering how he could make her want so badly with only a kiss. He wasn't unaffected. She felt him grow hard against her stomach. He groaned and pulled back, but still held her close.

"I guess I didn't totally ruin the mood, huh?"

"No chance of that," he said, then left.

BELLA HATED TO admit it because it made her feel like a lovestruck teenager, but the highlight of her day was when Graham called her. He'd called her the last three nights since they went out and they'd talked, for as long or short a time as he had between surgery and his other duties. On Wednesday, she'd just hung up with him when her phone rang again. It was Rex, she saw, looking at her caller ID.

"Hi, Rex."

"Hi, Bella. Want to take in a movie Friday night?"

"That sounds nice but I can't."

"How about Saturday then?"

"I can't. I'm dating someone, Rex." She should have broken it to him more gently, but he knew she'd never felt more than friendship for him.

For a long moment he didn't speak. "We went out Saturday night."

"I know. It just happened."

"Since Saturday night."

"Yes. I don't want to lose your friendship, Rex. But I don't think we should date. It might give Graham the wrong idea."

"Graham McBride. The doctor you told me about? I thought he flaked out on you."

"I thought so too, but I was wrong."

He muttered something obscene, which let her know he was really upset. He almost never cussed around her. "He's got a rep, you know."

"I know. We talked about it. You don't need to worry about me, Rex."

"I hope you know what you're doing."

So do I, she thought, ending the call.

Chapter Eight

G RAHAM STRIPPED OFF his surgical gown and tossed it in the hamper. His cap and gloves went into the trash. He squeezed the bridge of his nose. Damn, damn, damn. He hated losing a patient. He'd known from the beginning of the surgery that there was very little hope that his patient would pull through, but that didn't make his death any easier to take. And now he had to go tell the man's wife of sixty years that he was gone. She was a sweet elderly lady who'd told him that her husband was the love of her life.

The love of her life. She meant it. It was obvious in everything she did, everything she said. He couldn't imagine what that would feel like. He'd had a hard enough time with his divorce and Cynthia sure as hell hadn't been the love of his life.

After he told her, and she went with her daughter to see her husband, he changed into his street clothes and left the hospital to go to his apartment. He was still on call but he didn't have to be in the hospital unless there was a new case or one of his existing patients came in with a problem.

For the first time since Sunday, when he'd left Bella's apartment, he didn't want to call her. He didn't want to talk to anyone. No doctor liked to lose patients but it was an inescapable part of medicine. Particularly surgery. Yet for some reason, this one had hit him especially hard.

But he knew Bella would be expecting his call, so he made it, thinking he'd hang up as quickly as he could. When it rang several times, he thought he might luck out and leave a message but she picked up.

"Graham, hi."

"Hi. I can't talk long. I just wanted to say hi."

"What's wrong?"

Did he sound that bad? Probably. "It's been a rough day."

"I'm sorry. Is there anything I can do?"

"No. Thanks."

"Do you want me to come over? If you want to talk—"

"No." He winced, knowing he sounded abrupt. "I'm crappy company right now."

"I understand. When I have a bad day, I don't want to see anyone either."

"Thanks. It's not you. It's just been a really shitty day."

"That's okay, Graham. You don't have to explain any further. I get it. But if you want to talk just call me. Okay?"

"Okay. Bella? I'll see you tomorrow."

"All right. Do you like lasagna?"

"Who doesn't?"

"Good. I'm cooking then."

"You don't have to cook for me."

"I don't have to. I want to. See you then."

Bella hadn't been annoyed with him. He could tell. She

does get it, he thought. Not only that, but she was cooking for him. Damn, what a woman.

"I'M NOT NERVOUS," Bella told herself in the mirror Saturday evening.

Oh, yeah? Then why is your stomach doing flip-flops?

I'm excited, she told her annoyingly accurate inner voice. *There's a difference.*

Her doorbell rang and she went to answer it. Expecting Graham, she was surprised when she saw who stood there.

"Rex? What are you doing here?" She knew she'd told him about Graham. And she remembered turning him down when he'd suggested they go out again.

"I was in the neighborhood and decided to stop by. Are you going to let me in or keep me standing on your doorstep?"

Reluctantly, she stepped aside to let him in. What game was he playing?

"What smells so good? Is that your lasagna?"

"Yes. What's going on, Rex?"

"I love lasagna." He walked over and sat on the couch, smiling at her engagingly. Abby wandered in and jumped up beside him to be petted.

Bella liked Rex. She enjoyed his company and considered him a friend. But that was all. He was good-looking, he treated her well and she knew other women thought she was crazy not to get together with him. But there was no zing there. Her blood didn't sizzle and her legs had stayed firmly beneath her the few times she'd kissed him.

Unlike with Graham. He only had to look at her a certain way and she needed to fan herself.

"Don't get comfortable. I have a date."

"With that doctor you told me about?"

"Yes."

He leaned back, stretching his arm across the back of the couch. Continuing to pet Abby with his other hand, he said, "I hear he's a player."

"How is that any of your business?"

He shrugged. "We're friends, aren't we? I'm just looking out for you." He continued to pet Abby, who looked about as blissful as a cat could look.

"Well, don't. I can take care of myself. You need to leave."

"Are you afraid to introduce me to your new boyfriend?"

Baffled, she stared at him. "What is with you? You've never acted like this before and I've had other dates."

"None that mattered."

She hadn't gotten to know Rex until after she and Cody broke up. So he had a point. But how did he know?

"This is different, isn't it?"

Her doorbell rang, sparing her from replying. "That's Graham and your cue to leave."

He didn't move. She sighed irritably and opened the door.

"Hi. You look great."

"Thanks." He walked in, handing her a six-pack of beer.

He stopped when he saw Rex and said, "I didn't realize you had company."

"I don't. He's leaving." Rex stood but still didn't move away from the couch. Bella gritted her teeth and introduced them. "Graham, this is Rex. Rex, this is Graham." The two men nodded at each other but made no move to shake hands.

"I'd love a beer. Thanks," Rex said.

"You're not getting one," Bella snapped, her patience exhausted. "Go away, Rex."

"Wow, that's not very friendly," he said, but he walked toward her.

"I'm not feeling very friendly," she said, all but shoving him out the door.

"He doesn't seem like your type," Rex said.

She slammed the door in his face without answering. What had gotten in to him? He'd never acted...well, jealous was the only word she could think of.

"Sorry about that," she said when she turned around.

"I know it's a cliché, but you look beautiful when you're mad."

She laughed, which she knew had been his intention. "Thanks for the beer. I'll get us both one."

Graham followed her into the kitchen. "What was that about? Or should I ask?"

She put the six-pack in the refrigerator and got two bottles out. "You can ask, but I have no idea." She found her bottle opener and pried off the caps. "That was my very irritating friend Rex." She handed him a beer bottle.

"Friend?"

"Friend," she said firmly.

"Does he know that?"

"He should. I've told him often enough." After setting down her beer, she opened the refrigerator and got out the salad.

"Tell me something, Bella. Do you think I'm not your type?"

She looked at him over her shoulder as she tossed the salad. "You heard that, huh?"

"Oh, yeah. I'm sure I was meant to hear it."

Bella walked over to him and took his beer, setting it on the counter. She slipped her arms around his neck, rose on her tiptoes and kissed him. For a moment he hesitated, but then he gathered her close and kissed her back. Their tongues touched, retreated, plunged deeper. Before she knew it, she was plastered against him, his hands on her butt bringing her even closer. He kissed her fiercely, as passionately as she kissed him. She let her head fall back and his lips traced her jaw, then moved on to her neck. She felt his hand on her breast and arched into him, wanting more.

Something dinged. She ignored it, being far more interested in the sensations Graham was arousing with his hand kneading her breast. It dinged again. And again.

"Um, that's the timer. I need to take the lasagna out of the oven."

He let her slide down his body, wringing a groan from both of them. "I think we answered that question," she said, smoothing down her skirt.

"What question?"

"You're definitely my type."

Chapter Nine

"DINNER WAS FANTASTIC," Graham said, picking up his plate and taking it to the sink. He decided there wasn't anything Bella couldn't do well if she set her mind to it. Except dance, he remembered with a smile.

"I wouldn't go that far but I'm glad you liked it. You sound surprised."

"Not surprised. Appreciative." He started rinsing off his plate.

"You don't need to do that."

"You cooked. The least I can do is put the dishes in the dishwasher. Besides, my mother would have my hide if I didn't help with the dishes."

"Does your mother cook a lot?"

"Some. She runs the cattle operation, though, which keeps her busy. We learned to pitch in from the time we could walk. And we all learned to cook. Well, except for Jessie."

"Your sister can't cook?"

"Not worth a damn. But she works magic with horses."

They finished washing up and went into her living room. Even considering the kiss earlier that night, Graham wasn't sure if Bella was ready to make love. And he didn't want to push her, even though there was nothing he wanted more than to make slow, sweet love to her all night long. Or fast. Fast would be good, too.

Hell, any way it happened would be good with him.

He sighed. "Did you want to watch a movie? Or we can go out to the theater if you want."

"No." She walked to him, looked up into his eyes and smiled. "I think we should finish what we started earlier."

He grinned. "Much better idea." He kissed her, pulled back and said, "You're sure?"

"Very," she said, and kissed him. He swept his tongue inside her mouth slowly, deliberately. She tasted sweet. Tangy. Spicy. And packed a hell of a punch.

He picked her up and she wrapped her legs around him. Slipping his hands underneath her skirt, he encountered the smooth, silky, bare skin of her ass. *She's wearing a thong.* He trailed kisses along her jawline, down to her neck, all the while caressing her gloriously naked skin.

She was wrapped around him, her sex snug up against his cock, her arms looped around his neck. She felt so good he could have gone off right then without any trouble. But he wanted more. He wanted to feast on her, have her come apart in his arms, hear her cry out when he buried himself inside of her. And that required a bed.

As he carried her to the bedroom, Bella unbuttoned his shirt, stringing kisses along his jaw while she did so. "Hurry," she said.

When they reached her bedroom, he set her on her feet

by the bed while they began shedding their clothes. He tossed his shirt aside and watched as she pulled off the silky shirt she wore and dropped it beside her. She unzipped her skirt and stepped out of it, leaving her wearing a siren-red push-up bra and tiny thong panties. And siren-red heels with straps that wrapped around her ankles.

"Damn," he said. "Talk about lucky."

She smiled and traced a hand down his chest to his belt, unbuckled it, then went to work on his pants. Once she had those undone, she opened the drawer of her bedside table. While she rustled around in there, he sat on the bed to take off his shoes and socks, but left his pants and boxers on.

"I bought a box of these today," Bella said, holding up a condom before tossing it on the bedside tabletop.

"Good, because one won't be enough." He sat on the bed, waiting for her.

"Promises, promises." Then she put a foot on the bed and bent down to loosen the straps around her ankles. Sending him a provocative glance over her shoulder, she asked, "Would you like to help?"

He looked at her leg, propped up on the bed. Bare, creamy smooth skin from ankle to hip. "Absolutely." Slowly, he unwrapped the ankle strap and took off her shoe. Tossing it aside, he patted the bed beside him. "Other foot." She put it up there and he repeated the process, wondering how the simple act of taking off her shoes could be such a turn-on.

Still standing in front of him, she reached behind her to undo her bra. She slid each strap slowly off her shoulders, then let it fall. Graham sucked in his breath when he saw her bare breasts. Full and beautiful, with tight pink nipples begging to be touched. He cupped one, fondled it, then licked and sucked her nipple while she put her hands in his hair to hold him close. He moved to her other breast and gave it the same treatment, then drew back to look at her breasts, her nipples hard points gleaming with moisture from his tongue.

He tumbled her onto the bed and came down on top of her. Kissed her long and deep until they were both panting. Bella cupped him through his pants and said, "Take these off."

Needing no further encouragement, he stood beside the bed and watched her eyes darken as he pushed his pants and boxers down and off. She held out her hand and he took it, grabbing a condom before coming down beside her. He slid his hand down over her smooth stomach and delved beneath the scrap of lace covering her. She was warm, wet and waiting for him. He slipped a finger inside her, drew it out and did it again. He added his thumb to rub her clit. He continued until she writhed, getting more turned on by the moment. He kissed her mouth, all the while continuing to pleasure her with his fingers. She bucked, gasped his name and he felt her convulse around his fingers. He almost came right then.

Ripping open the packet, he rolled the condom down over his cock. Parting her legs, he tried to enter her slowly, but she wrapped her legs around his hips and urged him inside. He drove inside her, again and again, the sounds she made while he did making him harder if possible. Each time he thrust into her, she raised her hips and met him, her muscles squeezing tight around him until she came again and he could hold back no longer. He came with a harsh groan, feeling as if the top of his head had come off. He barely managed to roll over so he didn't squash her, bringing her to lie on top of him. She looked down at him, an extremely satisfied smile curving her lips. He put his hand in her soft, silky hair, tugged her head down and kissed her.

He'd had good sex before. Even amazing sex. But nothing he'd ever experienced had been quite like making love to Bella. If he hadn't been so completely satiated, he might have worried. He still didn't want a long-term relationship, but if anyone could change his mind about that, it was Bella.

BELLA HAD ALMOST fallen asleep on top of Graham when she heard a phone ringing. It sounded like a landline. Which she didn't have. She raised her head. "What the—"

"Crap," Graham said.

Bella rolled off of him. Their eyes met. "Is that—?" she asked.

"My phone? Yes. It's the hospital." He reached over the side of the bed and pulled his phone out of the pocket of his pants. "Sorry. I have to answer this." He swiped it and still lying down, held it up to his ear. "Dr. McBride." He paused and listened. "Yes. No." He sat up and swung his legs over the side of the bed. "Right. I'll be there in ten minutes."

"Crap," he repeated. He stood and said, "I'm really sorry

but I have to go to the hospital. One of my patients is having problems." He picked up his pants and strode to the bathroom, giving her a bird's-eye view of as fine a male backside as she'd ever seen.

She heard the toilet flush, the water running and then he emerged from the bathroom, his mind already on his patient, if she had to guess. After picking up his clothes, he left the room. Bella searched in her dresser for a nightshirt and found one that was fairly new, pulling it on over her head. She went out into the living room to see he had his shoes and socks on and was wearing his shirt and buttoning it. *So this is what it's like to date a doctor. Even when they're off, they're not totally free.*

He stuffed his shirt in his pants and buckled his belt. He closed the space between them, leaned down and kissed her. "This wasn't how I wanted the night to end."

"Me either. But I'd have been a lot more unhappy if they'd called half an hour earlier."

"Good point. That's a very good point." He kissed her again, briefly, rubbed her arm and opened the door. "I'll call you."

Promise? She wanted to ask, but didn't because that would sound pathetic. Or needy. Or something she didn't intend to sound like. What it *wouldn't* sound like was the strong, independent woman she actually was.

Damn. This really blows.

She went to the couch to pet Abby, but her cat was having none of it. Abby jumped off the couch and darted away. *Damn it. Even the cat left me.*

Bella went back into her bedroom and stood beside the bed, remembering what it had felt like to be plastered up against Graham with her skirt pulled up and his hands on her butt. All over her butt. Shaking off the memory, she put on her favorite soft flannel pajama pants and crawled into bed, determined to sleep.

An hour later she was still awake when her phone vibrated with a text message. It was in sleep mode, which meant it didn't chime from eleven to seven a.m. Graham. She smiled.

ARE YOU AWAKE?

YES. HOW IS YOUR PATIENT?

DOING BETTER NOW. SENT HIM HOME.

ARE YOU STILL AT THE HOSPITAL?

IN MY TRUCK IN THE PARKING LOT. SORRY I LEFT SO QUICKLY.

YOU'RE FORGIVEN. PATIENTS COME FIRST.

There was a long pause. Then another text came through.

YOU ARE A GODDESS.

LOL. WHY? B/C I'M NOT MAD?

THAT. AND OTHER THINGS. ☺

WANT TO COME OVER?

YES. THERE IN FIVE.

"He's coming back," she told Abby. Grinning, she was sure, like a crazy person. Apparently, Abby was still pissed at her. She glared at Bella and stalked off. "Be like that," Bella called after her. "He's still coming over."

A few minutes later she opened the door. He scooped her up in his arms and kissed the bejesus out of her. "Wait," she said when he started for the bedroom. "I have to lock the door." He turned around and let her lock it. By the time they reached her bedroom, she was naked and he was close to it.

"And now," he said, tossing her on the bed. "About those other things…"

Chapter Ten

H E LIKED HER. Really liked her. Probably too much. But right now, lying in Bella's bed with her snuggled up against him, and feeling more satisfied than he'd been in far too long, he couldn't bring himself to worry. Things had a way of working themselves out.

"Do you have to work Monday?" he asked her.

"No. We're traditional. We work Saturdays and close on Mondays. Do you?"

"Yes. But I'm free that night. Can I take you to dinner?"

"No, but you can pick up pizza and bring it over here."

"Pizza sounds good. What do you like on it?"

"Anything but anchovies and jalapeños. Surprise me. But there's still Sunday to talk about. Unless you have to work."

"I have to make rounds but then I'm all yours."

"I like the sound of that." She kissed him and things were just heating up when a very loud meow came from behind the closed door of her bedroom.

"Sounds like Abby wants in," Graham commented.

Bella rose onto her elbow and said, "Do you mind?"

"Of course not. It's her home, isn't it?"

She grinned. "You'd be surprised how many people don't

get that."

"I like cats. And dogs. And horses. And other critters. I grew up on a ranch, remember?"

"I guess you did have lots of animals. It's just…you're not a cowboy at all." She got up and put on his shirt.

"I used to be," he said, admiring her. There was something about a beautiful—and naked—woman that made him thankful he was male. And straight.

"You used to be a cowboy? You're kidding. When?"

"In high school. My brothers and I all were, for a few years. And Jessie is a cowgirl, through and through."

"I just can't see you as a cowboy."

"We grew up in Central Texas on a ranch. Almost everyone around here was involved with the rodeo at one time or another."

Bella opened the bedroom door. "What was your event? Or events?"

The cat stalked in and glared at him. Then she turned and glared at Bella, meowing with an angry huff. She jumped up on the bed and hissed at Graham.

"Whoa there, Abby. I like cats." He held out a non-threatening hand. Abby took a swipe and he pulled it back barely in time.

"Abby, what's the matter with you? This is Graham. You know him. He won't hurt you." She walked over and put a hand on the cat's head. Abby shrugged her off. "Are you sure you like cats?"

"I like cats fine. But I don't think your cat likes me anymore." Abby lashed her tail as if to say "you bet your ass, I don't."

"She goes to the shop with me a lot. She usually likes everyone."

Oh, yay. Everyone but him, apparently. "Was she a rescue?"

"Not officially but she was a stray who adopted me when I moved to town."

"Maybe I remind her of someone who mistreated her."

Bella was frowning, looking at the two of them. Then her brow cleared. She held out her hand to the cat and yanked it back when Abby swiped at it. "She's jealous. She doesn't approve of me having a sex life."

"How do you know that's it?"

The cat sprang down from the bed and left after giving them a disgusted glance.

"Because she was fine until she saw us in bed together. She let you pet her the first couple of times you came over. She's been mad at me ever since you left earlier. Plus—" She hesitated, looked away, then met his gaze. "She did this once before, with a man I was involved with when I first came to town."

"Great," he said sarcastically.

"If it's any consolation, she was worse to him than she is to you."

"It's not. But you could console me."

"Oh, really? How do I do that?"

"You can start by taking off that shirt."

She smiled and began to unbutton the shirt.

MONDAY GRAHAM RAN into Turner, who was on his way out of the hospital as he was headed in. They stopped to talk for a minute. "Are you going to the American Cancer Society fund-raiser dinner next Saturday?" Turner asked Graham.

"Crap. I'd forgotten about that. I paid for a table but I didn't plan on being there." Graham was happy to donate to a good cause, and God knows cancer research was a good cause, but he didn't figure they needed him to be there in person. Black tie. Boring. Lots of people making small talk.

"Yeah, well, tough. We both have to go."

"Why?"

"Because I got cornered by the mayor and said I'd be there, so I threw you under the bus too."

"Thanks a lot."

"You're welcome. Happy to help." He paused and said, "Why do you look so happy?"

"Do I?"

His brother eyed him for a long moment. "Hell, you got laid."

Well used to his brother by now, Graham said, "If I did, it's none of your business."

Unsurprisingly, Turner ignored him. "Who is she? Oh, wait. It's Bella Benson."

"Yes, it's Bella and no, you aren't getting any details."

"Hell, I haven't had sex with a woman in months. You could at least talk about it so I could live vicariously."

"Not happening, Turner." But if he was going to de-

EVE GADDY

scribe the weekend, he'd say it had been great. Fantastic,
even. Lots of sex, amazing sex at that. They'd talked a lot
too. He'd enjoyed getting to know her better and hearing her
take on Last Stand. Which was: she thought it was a pretty
great place to live. Unlike his ex-wife, who had hated it when
he dragged her there, afraid he'd want to go back when he
finished his schooling. Which he had.

The only fly in the ointment was the fact that no matter
how he tried, Bella's cat still hated him. But he had a plan in
mind to change that.

"Oh, well, I tried. Are you going to take Bella to the
dinner?"

"Considering I just found out I was going—thanks to
my asshole brother—I don't know if she can make it. But
yes, if she can. Who are you taking?"

"I don't know," Turner said. "Since Crystal and I broke
up, I didn't really have anyone in mind."

"You and Crystal broke up months ago."

"True but I just haven't gotten back into the whole scene."

"Ask Charlie."

"Charlie?" Turner asked blankly.

"Yeah, Charlie. You know, the cute brunette who owns
the pie shop? About so high." Graham held out a hand about
shoulder height. "Pretty. Sweet. You've known her forever."

Turner scowled. "Charlie's dating that asshole, Wallace."

"She was dating him. I heard they broke up. I was in
Char-Pie the other day and I heard her telling someone. And
she didn't seem too heartbroken about it, either."

Turner perked up. "That's good news. I think I will ask her. Thanks, Graham."

"You're welcome. Although I should have let you twist in the wind."

LATER THAT EVENING Graham arrived at Bella's place with a large pizza known as *The Works* and a cat toy with a waving feather that the clerk at the pet store said was one of her top sellers. He didn't know if Abby would go for it, but while it didn't seem to faze Bella that her cat didn't like him, it bothered the hell out of him. Animals liked him. Dogs, cats, horses, cows. In fact, growing up, he'd been the only one who could manage to corral the barn cats for their shots. Not that it had been easy, but he'd managed to do it when no one else could.

Bella opened the door and took the pizza box he handed her. "Hi, come in. This smells good. What kind is it?"

"The Works. Minus anchovies and jalapeños."

"Perfect. What's in the bag?" she asked on her way to the kitchen.

She set the pizza down on the counter and Graham set his bag beside it. Then he pulled her to him for a kiss. Her lips were soft and warm and she responded readily. Regretfully, he kept it brief since they were both hungry. "I'll tell you about it after dinner. Let's go eat," he said. No sense in letting a good pizza go to waste.

Bella got out plates and napkins. "Monday is my day to

do everything I can't manage during the week. When I went to the store today, I picked up some beer. Do you want one?"

"If you're having one."

"Sounds good." She got out a couple of bottles and gave him one.

"What else did you do today?" Graham asked, twisting off the bottle top and taking a swig.

"I cleaned the shop, washed towels and smocks and got everything ready for next week. Then I came home and did laundry here. It was a very exciting day," she added dryly.

Graham laughed. "Sounds like it. Don't you have a service who can clean the shop?"

"Yes. It's called Bella's cleaning service. Seriously, I'd love to have one but they're too expensive."

He'd never thought about it but now that he did, he wasn't surprised. His cleaning lady wasn't cheap and his apartment, while not tiny, wasn't huge either. "Do you mind doing it?"

"Cleaning? Well, it's not my favorite thing but somebody has to do it." She took a bite of pizza and a swallow of beer. "How was your day?"

"It was good." They talked about what he'd done that day until they finished the pizza. After they cleaned up, which didn't take long, he said, "Before I forget—" He walked over to the countertop and picked up the plastic bag he'd brought along with the pizza. "This is for Abby."

"You brought Abby something? That was sweet."

He pulled the box out of the bag. "It's a toy."

She cocked an eyebrow. "So I see. Trying a little bribery?"

"Whatever works."

She looked doubtful but didn't say anything while he put the toy together. "Where is she?" he asked.

"Probably hiding in the bedroom. Come on." She went into the living room and called for the cat. Sure enough, Abby came out of the bedroom, took one look at Graham, arched her back and hissed.

Undeterred, Graham set the toy down and said, "It's called a feather whirl." He flicked the feather on a stick. "Look, Abby. It's fun." The cat sniffed disdainfully, as if to say, "That won't cut it, dude" and walked away. Okay, more like stalked.

"She might play with it later, once we're not looking or have left the apartment."

He thought he had on his poker face or "doctor" face, as his sister called the expression that gave nothing away, but apparently Bella saw right through that.

"Give her some time, Graham. She'll come around." She didn't add, "I hope" but she might as well have.

Graham could be patient when he needed to be. And he had more bribes, and was willing to keep them coming. He had no idea what was the way to a cat's heart, but he was going to experiment until he figured it out.

"You know it wouldn't bother me as much if I didn't know she hated the guy you used to date."

Bella laughed. "You're nothing like him. Besides, Abby didn't like him from the first. You, on the other hand, she liked—until you stayed over. She's used to having me all to herself when we're at home."

"As long as you don't take her dislike of me to heart I can deal."

"I won't."

"Maybe. But I know an 'if my cat doesn't like you, I don't like you,' person when I see one."

She smiled but shook her head. "Ordinarily, I'd say you're right. But it depends on the circumstances." Bella walked over and put her arms around his neck. She kissed him, slipping her tongue inside his mouth and pressing her body up against his. And just like that, he wanted her.

Oh, hell, she didn't need to do a thing but stand there and he wanted her. She took his hand and led him to the bedroom, losing her shirt along the way. Once there she helped him take off his shirt and pants, then smiled and pushed him onto the bed. Watching him, she took her sweet time unhooking her bra and letting it slide off her arms. He started to reach for her but she backed up and unbuttoned her jeans, then slid the zipper down, oh, so slowly. Just as slowly, she pushed them down her legs and peeled them off.

Graham groaned. She wore tiny pale pink panties…and nothing else. "You're killing me here," he said, his voice husky.

"That's the idea," she said, and let him pull her on top of him. And then she proceeded to completely blow his mind. Still wearing her panties, she rubbed against him, smiling when he grabbed her butt and pressed her close. She kissed him, slow and deep, and so damn sexy. She sat up, bringing her sex even more firmly against his cock, took his hands and placed them on her full breasts.

He indulged both of them, caressing her breasts, plucking at her nipples, then pulling her breasts close so he could lick and suck each nipple. He tried to hold back but he knew he was going to blow any moment, so he rolled her onto her back and stripped off her panties. He grabbed a condom, ripped open the package and put it on, then parted her legs and plunged inside her. She was tight. Wet. Wild. He pulled almost all the way out and drove inside her again. She hooked her legs around his hips and urged him faster. Faster still, as he thrust into her again and again, until she tightened around him and convulsed and he spilled himself deep inside her with a mind-melting climax.

Chapter Eleven

"CAN YOU STAY tonight?" Bella asked Graham later.

"I want to but I can't. I have a surgery tomorrow morning and my day will start early. I need to go home and get some sleep."

"Okay."

"I'm really sorry."

He sounded worried. Did he think she was going to yell at him for being conscientious about his work? "It's not a big deal, Graham. You have work. So do I."

"Still, thanks for understanding." He kissed her and went into the bathroom.

Bella got up and pulled on her T-shirt and panties. Abby came in, looking around cautiously. Then Graham came out of the bathroom and she took off.

Graham didn't say anything but she could tell by how his lips tightened that he wasn't happy.

After stuffing his shirt into his pants, he said, "I almost forgot, what are you doing next Saturday night?"

"Nothing after work. Why?"

"Want to go to a fund-raising dinner with me?"

"A what?"

"A fund-raising dinner. It's for cancer research."

"Oh, is it like the spaghetti dinner for Alzheimer's research?"

"Sort of. It's out at Jameson House."

"Jameson House? You mean the place where the hospital holds those fancy-ass parties?" Ruby Jameson was not only one of the main benefactors of the hospital; she'd also willed her family home to the hospital for their use. There were some stipulations, such as the historical character of the house had to be preserved, and it would remain hospital property and not be sold. The hospital board had voted to turn it into an event center as well as administrative offices for the hospital and a couple of charities. Bella had done clients' hair for a number of functions held there. Dressy functions. Very dressy.

Graham laughed. "That's the place. Can you go?"

"Is it casual?"

"Afraid not. Black tie. Is that a problem?"

Black tie? Black freaking tie? "No, no. That's fine." *No it's not, you idiot. You don't have anything anywhere close to a formal dress to wear.*

"If it is, I'm sure you can just wear a cocktail dress."

Bella stared at him, wondering if he could really be as dense as he seemed at the moment. She couldn't decide whether she was most irritated because it didn't occur to him she wouldn't have anything to wear or if it pleased her that he obviously thought she was successful enough to have a formal—a formal!—lying around.

"Don't worry about it. I'm sure I have something that

will work."

"Good. We'll talk about details later." She saw him to her door. He kissed her goodbye and said, "I'll talk to you tomorrow."

The instant the door closed behind him Bella texted her friend, Delilah.

ARE YOU AWAKE? I HAVE AN EMERGENCY.

WHAT KIND OF EMERGENCY?

A DESPERATE EMERGENCY.

NEVER MIND. CALL ME.

Bella speed-dialed her friend.

Delilah answered with, "What's going on? What's this emergency? Are you hurt?"

"No, not at all. I need a formal."

"A formal? You mean like a dress?"

"No, I mean like a raincoat."

Delilah laughed. Bella continued, "Yes, a formal dress. Do you have something I can borrow?"

"Yes, but why do you need it?"

"Graham asked me to go with him to a fund-raiser. A black-tie fund-raiser. I don't have a formal. Hell, I've only got two cocktail dresses, one of which isn't really a cocktail dress. It's more of a church dress. Why would I need a formal?"

"To go out with Graham, apparently. Obviously, things are going well. Can I say I told you so?"

Bella had talked to Delilah and Joey after her second date crisis. At that point, she'd wondered if she'd even be seeing

Graham again. They'd both told her not to worry.

"You did. And they are going well. Really well."

"Did you hook up?"

"What kind of question is that?"

"The obvious one," Delilah said dryly. "And I'll take that as a yes."

There was no point in not telling her friend. Besides, Bella wanted to talk to someone. "He spent Saturday and Sunday nights with me. And he came over tonight after work. But he left right before I called you. He has an early day tomorrow. I really like him, Delilah."

"That's great, Bella. I'm happy for you."

"Me too. Except…there's a problem."

"What kind of problem?"

"Abby."

"What about her?"

"She doesn't like him. It's not so much a problem for me. I mean, cats are like that sometimes. She's jealous. She liked him before he stayed over but now she doesn't."

"I don't think I'd let my cat run my love life. If she's jealous, she'll get over it."

"Tell that to Graham. It really bothers him. Especially after I told him she hated Cody."

"So did I. He was a jerk. But why would you tell Graham that?"

"It just slipped out. Graham brought her a present tonight when he came over. He's worried. He said I was an 'if my cat doesn't like you I don't like you' type person."

"He has a point. But there you go. If he was a jerk, he

wouldn't care. What did he get her?"

"A cat toy. A stick on a feather that moves around if she bats at it. She wouldn't touch it. I'm hoping she will when no one is here."

"What will you do if she doesn't come around?"

"Graham said he intends to keep working on her."

"It should be interesting to see who wins out. Now, what is this party you need the dress for?"

"It's a fund-raiser dinner for cancer research. At Jameson House."

"Whoa. Fancy. That place is beautiful. Come over tomorrow after work. I don't need to be at the restaurant early. I'll pull out a few things I think will work for you and you can try them on."

"You're a lifesaver. Thanks, Delilah."

"You're welcome. And I want more details when you come."

GRAHAM WAS DETERMINED to convince Abby that he was not a serial killer come to murder her mistress. He decided he'd drown the cat in presents until she had no choice but to like him.

He didn't analyze why it was so important for Bella's cat to like him. It shouldn't have been a big deal. But by God, he was going to win over that cat if it was the last thing he ever did.

Bella opened the door and he drew in his breath. A vision in blue. Her dress, a deep blue strapless gown that bared her creamy neck and shoulders, cinched in at the waist, and then flaring out, was shorter in the front and full length in the back. It was striking and unique.

As was her hair. Myriad shades of blue, dyed to match and blend with the dress. "Wow, you look amazing." He kissed her.

"You don't think it's too much?" she asked a little anxiously. "You know, with the hair and all?"

"Not on you." Another woman might be hard pressed to pull off the look, but Bella did it perfectly. "You're beautiful."

"Thank you. But I wasn't fishing. I haven't been to an event like this before. I wanted to make sure I look all right."

"More than all right," he assured her. "Where's Abby?" He motioned with the sack he held. "I have something for her."

"Another bribe?"

"I prefer to think of them as presents."

Bella grinned. "Oh, excuse me. A present is completely different."

"That's right." He pulled his recent offering out of the bag.

She called Abby. The cat came into the living room, gave Graham what could only be called a baleful glare, but she didn't run off. Yet.

The toy, a ball with holes in it where he'd stuffed treats, had looked like a sure-fire winner to him. He set it on the floor and said, "Here you go, Abby."

Cautiously, she walked over and sniffed the ball. Batted it once and then gave a disdainful sniff before darting away.

"I'm sorry," Bella said. "She's being a brat."

"Hey, she came over and touched it. That's more than she did with the other one. So, progress." He had more presents and it looked like he was going to need to use every one, and probably more. "Are you ready to go?"

"You're not going to make me dance, are you?"

"Bella, I wouldn't 'make' you do anything you don't want to do. But as it happens there's no dancing. No music, in fact. And—" He hesitated but decided to come clean. "The food will be good but the presentations and speeches are likely to be very boring."

"You don't sound like you want to go. Why are we going?"

"Turner got roped into it so he threw me under the bus too. But since you'll be there with me, I'm thinking it won't be too bad."

"I'm supposed to save you from being bored? Oh, great."

"Bella." He pulled her close and kissed her. "There's no way in hell I could be bored when I'm with you."

"That's sweet. But I hope you don't regret it."

"I won't," he said firmly. "Let's go."

Chapter Twelve

BELLA HAD HEARD about Jameson House but she'd never been there. A couple of her clients were administrators for charitable organizations that had offices at Jameson House and a few of her clients had been to the house for parties and fund-raisers.

One day when Bella was dyeing her hair, Clara Perkins had told her the history of Jameson House and the family it had belonged to. A Victorian farmhouse, it had been built in the early 1890s by the grandson of the original Gordon C. Jameson, who had been a survivor of the battle of Last Stand. Gordon C. Jameson III made his fortune in cattle and railroads, and when he married, he built the huge house for his bride, a city girl from New York. Ruby, the hospital benefactor, was Jameson III's spinster granddaughter and the only surviving member of her family.

It was a beautiful old house, perfectly maintained over the years. They were directed to the ballroom on the first floor. "You said this was a dinner, not a dance," Bella said in a loud whisper. "You promised I wouldn't have to dance."

He shot her an amused glance. "Relax. The ballroom is the only place big enough to seat everyone. There's no dancing, although you'll wish there was after listening to half a dozen people speak."

They walked into the ballroom to a burst of color. Large, round tables with white linen tablecloths were placed throughout the room. The centerpieces were bouquets of wildflowers with flickering votive candles on either side. The wood floor was a gorgeous light brown, buffed and shined to a beautiful glow. Flowers were the theme, with pots and hanging baskets of gaily colored flowers placed throughout the ballroom. In the very center of the room was a fountain, but instead of water it held flowers. Flowering vines fell from one level to another, pooling at the bottom in an explosion of color.

A beautiful brunette around Graham's age, wearing a low-cut, slinky, long red dress walked up to him. "Graham, I'm so glad you came." With a twinkle she added, "And here I heard a rumor that you weren't going to be here."

"Wouldn't have missed it," Graham said.

"How are you?"

"I'm good, Rebecca. You look great. How have you been?"

"Wonderful, thanks. I'm getting remarried in a couple of months and want you to come to the wedding."

"Congratulations. I'd love to come. Let me introduce you to—"

"No need," Rebecca interrupted. "You're Bella Benson." She took Bella's hands in hers. "I'm Rebecca St. James. I'm so pleased to finally meet you."

"It's nice to meet you," Bella said, a bit surprised at the

enthusiastic greeting.

Rebecca released her hands but continued to talk. "You look lovely. I adore your hair. I'd really like to do something different to mine."

"Thank you." Bella had been looking around and was pleased to see there were other women with fun, unusual hair colors there.

"I'm a three-year cancer survivor," Rebecca continued. "You styled my favorite wig. You're so talented and generous. I was beyond thrilled when Turner told me Graham was bringing you to the dinner tonight."

"I'm so glad you liked the wig," Bella said, pleased but a bit overwhelmed at the high praise. "My mother died from cancer. It seems like the least I can do."

"The least you can do?" Rebecca repeated in astonishment. "It's a wonderful, wonderful thing you do. Both that you're able to do it but also because you donate your time and abilities."

Graham looked mystified at the conversation. Rebecca turned to him. "Bella styles wigs for cancer survivors as a free service. I take it you didn't know?"

"No. She's never mentioned it." He gave Bella an intrigued glance. "Why didn't I know this?"

"It never came up."

"She's being modest." Rebecca turned back to Bella. "A friend of mine who's also a survivor said you styled her wig. She lives in Austin. Do you do this everywhere you live or how does that work?"

"Yes, I've been doing it for a long time. But the wigs

don't always go to the community I live in. I'm part of an organization that provides wigs free for cancer survivors who otherwise couldn't afford it, and they are nationwide. They also sell the wigs and the money goes to cover the organization's expenses as well as to those in need. Survivors in Style. Have you heard of us?"

"Oh, yes, that's one of my favorite charities. We'll have to hold a fund-raiser specifically for Survivors in Style."

They talked a little more and then Rebecca left them. "You're a woman of surprises," Graham said to Bella.

"Because I style wigs?"

"Because you do it for cancer survivors and donate your time and talent."

"It's not a big deal. I'm just happy to be able to contribute."

"Rebecca thought it was a big deal."

"She was being nice."

"Yes, and she is nice. But that doesn't mean you don't deserve credit for a beautiful thing you do."

Bella scowled at him. "You make me sound like a saint. I'm not. I have a knack with wigs and I like to do it."

"Ladies and gentlemen, if you'll take your seats we can get started," the mayor said, speaking into a microphone.

"This way," Graham said. "I saw our names at one of the tables that's close to the stage."

"Do you know who we're sitting with?"

Graham grimaced. "One of the couples is a doctor I know and his fiancée. I saw their place cards. I didn't see who the other couples were, so I might know them or I might not."

"I like to meet new people," Bella said. "Don't you?"

"Depends. Not usually at a dinner like this. To tell you the truth, I'd just as soon give money and not have to show up." He looked at Bella and smiled. "But it's a lot better than usual this time, no matter who we sit with."

"Why is that?"

"Because you're here with me."

Her breath caught. It was such a simple thing to say. But it made her feel special. And she liked that feeling a lot.

The rest of the evening passed more quickly than she'd thought it would. Their table of eight consisted of the two of them and three more couples. One was an older couple named Gus and Doris Edwards. They were very nice but Doris was hard of hearing and apparently had never heard of hearing aids. Gus repeated the conversation to her. Then there were two couples who looked to be around Graham's age, and Graham knew all of them. Mindy and George Spitzer were very nice and friendly. Phillip Cooper was the doctor Graham knew. He was nice, if quiet. His fiancée, Fern, was very pretty and very aloof. To Bella. To Graham, she was flirty and effusive.

"Where do you work, Bella?" Mindy Spitzer asked her. "At the hospital?"

"No. I'm a hairdresser. I own Bella's Salon here in town."

"Oh, how…interesting," Fern said, in a tone that meant anything but.

"I'll have to try your salon," Mindy said, directing a

EVE GADDY

quelling glance at Fern. "I've been going over to Fredericksburg but I'd love to be able to go to a salon here in town."

"We have several hairdressers and would love to have you come in," Bella said. "And you too, of course, Fern," she added sweetly.

Fern seemed about to speak but Phillip said quietly, "Fern."

Fern rolled her eyes but didn't say anything.

"You're that new gal Dotty Allen talks about," Doris announced in the loud tones of the hard of hearing. "Your hair is blue. I like it."

"Thank you," Bella said. "I like to experiment. Dotty has been very kind about recommending my salon to people."

"My mother had blue hair. But not like yours. We used to call them the blue-haired ladies." She laughed. "Nowadays you have all kinds of colors. Wish my mother was alive to see it."

Bella didn't know how to respond to that but luckily was saved by the mayor announcing the first speaker. Graham reached for her hand and smiled at her.

Was it ridiculous that she felt her heart go pitter-patter simply from holding his hand?

Chapter Thirteen

"I THOUGHT THAT thing would never end," Graham said on the way to Bella's apartment. "Did you hate it?"

"Did I hate what?" Bella asked.

"The dinner."

"Of course not. Why would I hate it? It was very nice, and for a good cause."

"It was boring."

"Not all of it. The survivors' stories were inspiring."

"True. But listening to the researcher was worse than reading a medical textbook. Much worse. At least the textbooks are understandable."

Bella chuckled. "Since I've never read one, I wouldn't know, but I'll admit his talk went over my head. The Spitzers were nice," she added. "And so were Doris and Gus. She cracked me up."

"What did you think of Fern?"

She debated whether to hedge but decided she might as well be honest. To some extent, anyway. "She wasn't very friendly. To me." But she sure as hell had been to Graham.

"Yeah, Fern's a little hard to take sometimes."

"Did you date her?"

He shrugged. "Not for long. Did she say something to upset you?"

"Why do you ask that?"

"Because when you and she came back from the bathroom, she was smirking and you looked upset."

Bella shrugged. "Not upset. Just annoyed. She said something catty about my shop." Which she had, but that wasn't what had bothered Bella. She'd been surprised when Fern had gone to the restroom with her but not for long.

"I know you won't mind a little constructive criticism, Bella," Fern had said in a sticky-sweet voice. "Have you thought about giving your little shop a bit of a face lift? With it being on Main Street, we want to present our best side to the public, don't we?"

Bella had simply stared at her.

Fern looked in the mirror to put on her lipstick. "I was surprised to see you with Graham tonight."

"Oh, really? Why?" She knew she shouldn't have answered but Fern was pissing her off.

Fern laughed lightly. "You're hardly his type. You've heard he's going to be chief of surgery once Dr. Prior retires, haven't you?"

"No, I hadn't heard that."

"Oh, yes. It's all but decided. Unless something happens to make the powers that be decide otherwise."

"What would happen that might make them change their mind?"

"Why, I have no idea. But it's a prestigious position.

Graham is so well suited for the role."

And you are not.

No, Fern didn't say that but it had sure as heck been implied. She shook her head, trying to dispel the memories.

"Do you want to talk about it?" Graham asked.

"What, Fern's insult? She was just needling me. I blew it off." She'd blown off the comment about the shop. But about Graham, she admitted that had struck a nerve. Still, Graham had told her from the first he wasn't looking for a long-term commitment. So what difference did it make if Bella was his type...or if he was hers, for that matter?

Bella leaned across the console and kissed him. "I have a much better idea of what we should be doing rather than talking about obnoxious people."

"What's that?" He cupped her face in both hands, tracing a thumb over her lips.

"Let's go inside and I'll show you."

He kissed her and released her. "I like the way you think."

THEY BARELY MADE it inside before they were in each other's arms. Graham kicked the door shut behind them, then backed her up against it and kissed her. He'd taken off his jacket but he still had on all kinds of clothes she had no idea how to get him out of. So she started with his tie. Her fingers fumbled but she finally got it untied and managed to wrestle open his top button.

Meanwhile, Graham kissed his way along her jaw, to her neck, down to her shoulders, pressing hot kisses wherever her skin was exposed. "I wanted to do this all night. All that soft silky skin just waiting to be touched." He traced a finger along the top of her bodice. "Kissed," he said, and kissed his way where his fingers had just stroked.

She moaned and reached for his shirt. Wrestled more of the buttons free. Graham yanked the shirttails out of his pants and finished unbuttoning his shirt. He stripped it off while kissing her again, his tongue tracing her lips, slipping inside her mouth to tangle with hers. She felt his hands delve into her bodice and fondle her breasts. The ache between her legs grew and spread until it was a throbbing demand.

She heard a sound. Heard it again. Through the sensual haze she realized Abby was meowing. Pitifully. She turned her mouth to the side and tried to catch her breath. "Wait."

"What's wrong?" His voice was husky, his breathing hard.

"It's Abby. I hear her but I don't see her."

He cocked his head to listen. If he sighed, it was so slight that she couldn't honestly say he had.

"You're right." He let her go and looked around. "I don't see her either."

The meows became more frantic. "I'm sorry," Bella said. "She sounds like she's hurt. Or scared."

"You're right, she does. Don't worry, we'll find her."

They both started looking around, moving toward where they believed the sounds came from.

"There she is," Graham said, pointing to a bookshelf in

the living room. "She's on the very top. Could she be stuck?"

Bella looked up. "I don't know. I guess she could be too frightened to come down. But she hasn't ever done this before."

"Cats get stuck in trees, don't they?"

"I suppose. But since she adopted me, she always stays inside, so I really don't know."

Graham walked over to the shelf and looked up at the cat. "Here, Abby. Here, kitty."

Bella went to him and added her voice. Abby was having none of it. She continued to meow, more and more plaintively. "I'll get a step stool," Bella said, and went off to find one.

When she returned Graham was holding a treat out and talking soothingly to Abby. "You could save us all a lot of trouble by coming down now, you know," she heard him say. Abby meowed and showed her teeth, as if to say, "No freakin' way."

"It's not very high," Bella said, carrying a small step stool over to the bookcase. "But it's all I could find. Someone borrowed my other one and hasn't returned it." But this one wouldn't be anywhere near tall enough to help her. "I should probably use a chair."

Graham looked at the chair she indicated, then back at her. "Let me try first. I should be able to reach her." He took the stool from her and set it beside the very tall bookshelf. He climbed up on it and held the treat out again. "Come on, Abby. That's a good kitty."

"She looks interested," Bella said. "Look, she's moving

closer to you."

"How can you tell?"

Abby reached out a paw and swiped the treat from his palm.

"That's a girl." To Bella he said, "Can you get me another treat or three?"

She picked out another treat from the ball and handed it to him. "Maybe you should just hold out the ball."

"I'll try that if this doesn't work."

It took him another twenty minutes, but Graham was surprisingly patient with her cat. He alternated offering her treats and holding out the ball, while she very slowly crept closer. Once she got close enough to grab, Bella thought that's what Graham would do, but he didn't. He just kept offering treats, talking to the cat soothingly and waiting for her to decide to trust him.

Bella was absolutely charmed watching him. And quite a bit turned on seeing Graham, shirtless, wearing only his tux pants and convincing her cat to let him rescue her.

And he hadn't even gotten mad when Abby had totally disrupted their plans. Bella knew for a fact that Graham had been as hot as she was. And if she was frustrated, she couldn't imagine how he'd felt. But if he'd been angry or annoyed, he hadn't let it show.

Finally, Abby allowed him to pick her up and bring her down from the shelf. She even stayed in his arms for a bit while he petted her and talked to her. "There you go, sweetheart. You're safe now."

"My hero," Bella said, not really joking.

He gave her a self-deprecating grin. "Happy to be of service." He handed Abby over.

Bella petted her and scolded her, then took her to the kitchen to get her some kibble. Though she didn't really need it, after the gazillion treats Graham had just given her. After she got Abby settled, she went back to the living room. Graham had put on his shirt and was buttoning it.

"What are you doing?"

"Leaving?"

"Oh, no, you're not."

"I'm not? I figured the mood had been ruined and—"

"Are you kidding?" She walked up to him and unbuttoned his shirt again. Then she pushed it off his shoulders and took his hand to lead him to the bedroom. "I'm not sure I've ever been as hot as I am right now."

Graham blinked. "You're—hot? Really?"

"Absolutely. Seeing how sweet and patient you were with Abby—" She pushed him back until the backs of his knees bumped the bed and he sat. "It made me so happy that you cared enough to do what you did." She unzipped her dress and slowly peeled herself out of it. The bra was built into the dress so she only wore her panties and her high-heeled sandals. Remembering the dress was borrowed, she picked it up and draped it carefully over a chair then turned around to see him staring at her.

"It…uh…wasn't…"

"Wasn't what?"

"I can't remember."

Bella laughed and pushed him onto his back. Then she

climbed on top and kissed him. Hard.

He wrapped his arms around her and he kissed her back, tongues dueling, hands grappling. Graham flipped her onto her back and ranged himself above her. He kissed her, ran his hands deliberately down her body, stripped off her panties in a quick move. Bella tried to undo his pants but he brushed her away. So she slid her hand down and cupped him, then stroked the hard ridge of his arousal.

He sucked in a breath and groaned. He stood and stripped off his pants, reached for a condom and started to put it on. Bella held out her hand. "Let me," she said huskily. He handed it to her, watched as she rolled it down over his cock.

He started to come down on top of her but she said, "Let me," again and he lay down on his back. He reached for her, grasping her hips to help situate her. She guided him inside herself, her eyes locked on his. Then she began to rock. She rode him hard and fast, loving it when his hands came up to cup and caress her breasts.

Bella slowed her pace, loving it when he said, "You're killing me here."

"That's the point," she told him, but took pity on him and increased her speed. She closed her eyes and threw back her head, gasping as his fingers slipped between them and pushed her to a shattering crescendo. Moments later she felt him come, heard him gasp her name. He pulled her head down to kiss her and she collapsed on top of him, her heart still beating madly, her body still tingling from the aftereffects of amazing sex.

As she lay there wrapped in his arms, cocooned in the warm glow of contentment, she wondered whether what she felt might be more than sexual pleasure.

Could it be love?

No, of course not. Because that would be a disaster. She liked him. She liked him a lot. But love was not in the cards. Even if Bella was willing to risk it, Graham clearly had no serious intentions.

And then there was the matter of Graham becoming chief of surgery. The idea that she could be an obstacle to that happening bothered her. She didn't want to think that it mattered, but what did she know about hospitals and their hierarchy? Damn Fern for putting that thought in her mind.

⚕

LYING IN BED with his arm around Bella, thoroughly spent from making love, brought Graham a strange feeling of contentment. He didn't often feel that way with women. He didn't know why. To be honest, he wasn't sure he'd ever felt this content. This…happy. Which frankly, scared the hell out of him.

"Did she break your heart?"

"Who?"

"You know who."

Talk about busting wide open that postcoital glow. Graham started to brush her off but something prodded him to answer her. Maybe because no other woman had asked him about his ex in quite that way. They'd wanted to know what she was like, was he done with her, how long had it been since the divorce. That sort of thing, but not how had he *felt* about the whole thing.

"I thought she did. At the time."

"But now you're not sure?"

He shook his head. "No, I'm not sure. It's been ten years since we divorced. Longer since we were happy. Mostly I just remember being glad it was over. I was in my residency and I had enough to deal with. I worked pretty much constantly. Or it seemed like it." Work, eat, sleep. That's what he'd done for most of those years. It hadn't left a lot of time or energy for a serious relationship. Certainly not a marriage, as Cynthia had let him know, over and over.

"I know why I'm not in the market for a long-term relationship," Bella said, "but I don't know why you feel that way. Other than the bare fact that you're divorced."

"I'll tell you mine if you tell me yours," he said flippantly.

"All right." She sat up in bed, naked, with the sheet pooled around her lower body. "Want me to go first?"

Looking at all that naked perfection—her breasts were high and full, with pink-tipped nipples, her waist small, her hips curvy, and her legs, he knew, long and shapely—made him wonder why the hell they were talking about the past when they could be having fantastic sex right now.

"Eyes up here." She pointed to her own eyes, obviously reading his mind.

Graham grinned, reached out and tweaked a nipple. "Hard to do in the face of so much perfection."

"Flattery won't work." She got out of bed and walked over to her dresser, opened a drawer and pulled out a button-down soft cotton top. Shrugging into it, she buttoned it up as she walked back to him. "There."

"You're still distracting." Bella's face was as pretty as the rest of her. Delicate features, huge brown eyes, plump, full lips. Her hair spread about her shoulders, the myriad blue colors striking against the paleness of her skin. "You are so pretty." And completely nude beneath the shirt.

"Thank you, but that's not the subject." She settled back against the headboard. Graham sat up and settled against the headboard as well.

"I told you a little about the one I fell for when I first came to town. The one Abby hated. Cody. He was a cowboy who couldn't keep it in his pants. Once I figured that out, we were done."

"Sounds like good riddance."

"It was. But there was also my first love. A couple of years after my folks died, I met a guy. I was living in Austin and a friend introduced us at a party. We hit it off, started dating, and before we knew it, we grew pretty serious. Or at least I did."

"Him not so much, huh?"

"You got it. But I was crazy about him. So I dealt with it. He wasn't dependable to start with and over time, he grew even less dependable."

"Does he have a name?"

"Sebastian Grant. He was in college at the University of Texas. I thought some of his flakiness was because he was busy with school. And I've always been independent. I didn't need or even want him around every second or anything like that. But he started blowing me off more and more. When I tried to talk to him, he'd say I was paranoid and nothing was going on. He was busy, yada, yada." She paused and rolled her eyes.

"Busy doing what?"

"That's what I wanted to know. I never found out for sure but I suspect he was busy hitting on other women."

The guy sounded like a turd. "Why did you fall for him?"

She shrugged. "The usual reasons, I guess. He was fun. He could be charming. And he was great-looking." Graham laughed. Bella frowned at him. "So sue me. I like good-looking men." She patted his cheek. "Like you."

Graham knew women found him attractive. But no one had ever come out and said it like that. "Thanks. I think." He grabbed her hand and kissed it. "Is that the only reason you like me?"

"Don't be silly. You're fun and charming too."

Unsure what to say, Graham simply stared at her. Bella burst out laughing. "I'm sorry, but you should see your face," she said when she gained control. She leaned over and kissed him. "You are also sincere, dependable, and very up-front. Which I appreciate. A lot."

Somewhat mollified, he asked, "So what happened with Mr. Undependable?"

"About what you'd expect." Their gazes met and she said, "I got pregnant."

"I take it he didn't step up."

"No. He demanded I 'get rid of it.' Said he wasn't even sure it was his kid, which was ridiculous since he knew damn good and well it was. I refused to have an abortion. After a couple of weeks, he got over his hissy fit and said he'd support the baby, but he wasn't happy about it, and he made sure I knew it. That lasted about a month. Then I had a miscarriage."

"I'm sorry. That must have been hard. Especially with no support from the father."

"It was. There's no doubt a baby would have complicated my life and God knows how I'd have managed to support us, but I wanted it. Sebastian, on the other hand, was delighted. Which he didn't even try to hide."

This time he said it aloud. "What a turd. What did you do?"

"I kicked his ass out right then and there."

"Good. I'm sorry you had to go through that."

"I am too. The doctor said it was just one of those things and not to worry. It shouldn't affect whether I could have another baby."

Whoa. Babies. How the hell had they started talking babies?

Bella punched him in the arm. "Relax. My clock isn't ticking and besides, you've already told me you were a poor risk for a long-term relationship."

"Sorry."

"You should be. After what I just told you? Not just one, but two men I really cared about turned out to be total jerks.

I'm not about to let myself be that vulnerable again."

"Never?"

"Never say never. But not anytime soon."

"All men aren't like him."

"I know that. But it still doesn't make me eager to have another serious relationship." She cocked her head. "That's a good thing, isn't it?"

It should be. Why did that bother him? Wasn't it exactly how he felt? Bella was only saying what he *should* have wanted to hear.

"Okay, Graham, now it's your turn."

Chapter Fourteen

Bella wasn't sure Graham would open up about his marriage. After all, she reminded herself once again, they weren't serious. More than friends with benefits, but still not serious. But she wanted to know more about him. Especially why he was so determined not to get involved with anyone. His ex must have done a real number on him.

"If it bothers you that much don't tell me. It's none of my business, really." Which was true, but she still wanted to know.

"No, I said I'd tell you." He glanced at her with a self-deprecating smile. "The problem is, I feel like a dumbass every time I think about it. And I don't like that feeling."

She blinked. "A dumbass is about the last thing I'd think you are."

"You haven't heard the story yet."

"True, but I bet you shouldn't be so hard on yourself."

He simply shrugged. "Cynthia and I met when I was in med school. She was in college. We got married my third year of medical school. After college, Cynthia started law school. We were mostly okay at first. Then I started my internship and residency. She didn't deal with it well."

"Why?"

"Because I was gone all the time. And she was the type of woman who needed attention. And lots of it. She was a beautiful woman and she was accustomed to having men do whatever it took to get her to notice them. Apparently, simply loving her wasn't enough."

"But wasn't she studying and working a lot? If she was in law school—"

"She wasn't. She'd dropped out by then. I think it was more work than she wanted to do. But I could be wrong. I'm not exactly unbiased."

"I don't blame you."

"Cynthia became more and more dissatisfied. Nagged at me all the time because either I was gone or asleep." He paused and looked into Bella's eyes. "Which was basically true."

"Didn't she know that was how it would be during your schooling when you got married? I mean, you were in medical school."

"I thought she did but according to her, it was worse than she'd imagined. Which she told me whenever I managed to be home. And awake."

"So she didn't work?"

"She got a job as a legal secretary. She seemed to like it. She liked her boss, anyway." He gave Bella a sardonic look.

"Too much?"

"You could say that. One day I came home early—I don't remember why. And there she was, in our bed, with her boss. Who was also married, by the way."

Bella winced. "Ew. I'm sorry. What a shitty thing to do."

"Yep. I kicked him out, then Cynthia and I had a knockdown drag-out fight during which we both said a whole lot of things we shouldn't have. I packed a bag and left. We got a divorce not long after that."

Bella had a feeling there was a lot he wasn't saying. "Let me get this straight. She did this because you were working a lot? That was her excuse?"

"That's what she said. I 'wasn't putting anything into the marriage,'" he said, using air quotes.

"That doesn't make it right to cheat on you."

"That's what I thought. Cynthia, however, thought she was completely justified. So, that's my story."

"Because she cheated on you?"

"Partly. My career is demanding. Very. I'm not sure any woman would be willing to put up with my work."

She stared at him for a moment. He was serious. "That sounds like bullshit to me. Because your ex was a selfish tool, that means all women are? Then how come there are lots of doctors who are married and have been for a long time?"

"I didn't say all women. But there are a lot of divorces in the medical world."

"There are a lot of divorces in every profession. Cops are probably worse than doctors. Rock stars. Hollywood people. I could go on."

"How about we don't?"

He was looking irritated and she couldn't honestly blame him. "What would you like to do?" she asked, unbuttoning the top two buttons of the shirt she wore. Only the shirt.

His eyes darkened and he smiled. Damn, he had a great smile.

"Listen to music?" She popped the third button.

He shook his head.

"Have a drink?" Unbuttoned another.

Another shake of his head.

"I know. Get dressed and go to the movies?" The last three buttons went and she spread open the shirt.

"Not that either. I'm fairly certain you know exactly what I want to do." He tumbled her onto her back and settled between her legs. Then he kissed her.

Bella moaned and kissed him back, shoving her fingers through his hair. When he let her up for air she said, "Make love?"

"Ding, ding, ding. We have a winner."

"Yes we do," she said, wrapping her legs around his hips, her arms around his neck and kissing him again.

THE NEXT FEW weeks were among the best Graham could remember. He spent a lot of time with Bella. She didn't pout or get mad or try to make him feel guilty when he got called away. Not once. And it happened more than once. He had a hard time believing it didn't bother her but she swore it didn't. Maybe it was because she was busy, too, running a thriving business. From what he could tell, her salon was prosperous and kept her on the go. Sometimes she even bailed on him.

Cynthia had been like that. At first. Involved in her career, in her dreams. And then she'd changed.

Bella isn't Cynthia, he reminded himself.

At least the cat liked him now. He still brought Abby little gifts, but now he did so because he liked to see her get all excited rather than as a bribe.

One time he and Bella got on the subject of horses. Bella said she'd never ridden and would like to some day. Without telling Bella, he called Jessie.

"Hey, what do you have going Sunday morning?"

"Not much. Why?"

"Bella hasn't ever ridden. Can I bring her out to the ranch this Sunday?"

"Of course. Are you thinking of Dulce?"

Dulce was Jessie's old cutting horse mare who she used for people who'd never ridden before or for children. As her name suggested, she was sweet, gentle and placid. And very slow.

"Yes, she'd be great."

"I'll have to do some other things so I won't be able to hang around and help much. Will you be okay?"

"Will I be okay? I'm pretty sure I can handle teaching Bella to ride," he said dryly. "I've been riding since I was three. Longer than you, as a matter of fact."

Jessie laughed. "Just teasing. Sunday morning around ten?"

"Sounds good. Oh, in case you see her before that, it's a surprise."

"Got it. Hey, Graham?"

"Yeah?"

"I'm glad you and Bella are together. Don't screw this one up, okay? She's good for you."

"I'll see you Sunday," was all he said.

When he saw Bella Saturday night he said, "I have something planned for tomorrow. Are you free?"

"Sure. What are we doing?"

"It's a surprise. Wear jeans, boots, a hat and sunscreen." He looked at her, noting again how fair her skin was. "You might want a long-sleeved shirt too."

"I have to tell you, if you plan to take me hiking, forget it. I don't like hiking. And I don't have any hiking boots."

"You have cowboy boots. Those will do. Have you been hiking before?"

"Yes. It was hot and nasty and I got a lot of bug bites and I had to pee in the woods. It was only by the grace of God that I didn't get poison ivy on my bottom. So if that's the surprise, I'll have to decline."

Graham couldn't help laughing. "Poor baby. I promise if I ever take you hiking it will be cool and I'll make sure you don't pee in poison ivy."

"You're damn right you will, because I'm not going."

"Well, relax, because that's not the surprise."

After spending the night Saturday, Sunday morning he went back home to get dressed before picking her up. She held a ball cap in her hand but her hair was down and blonde. Just blonde. She must have washed it because the last he'd seen it, she'd had purple streaks. "I like your hair this way. I've never seen it all blonde. It's pretty." He toyed with a strand of it, running the silky stuff through his fingers.

"Meaning you don't like it when I color it."

"That's not what I said at all. I like your hair any way you want to wear it. Pink, purple, blue, whatever. It suits you. But there's no crime in saying I like it natural too."

"Okay, you get a pass."

Graham stopped to pet Abby and give her a squeaky mouse. "Be good. We'll see you later."

"You are so spoiling her."

He glanced at Bella and smiled. "Yeah. And your point would be?"

She rose up on her toes and kissed his cheek. "You're very sweet."

He raised an eyebrow. "Sweet?"

"Yes. Now, where are we going?"

"You'll find out."

⚕

GRAHAM WAS BEING stubbornly evasive about where he was taking her. Bella had tried everything she knew to find out what his plan was, but he simply smiled and said, "You'll find out."

"Isn't your family ranch north of town?" Bella couldn't remember who had told her that but she thought it was correct. And they were headed northwest of town.

"Hmm."

Since that was the fifth question she'd asked that he hadn't answered, she gave up and stared out the window.

Since she'd never been this far north of town, it was kind of interesting. They'd passed several ranches, or rather, signs pointing to ranches. Some she'd heard of, some she hadn't. Eventually Graham turned off the highway onto a county road and then off that road and drove through a large gate with an arch reading *McBride* and a sign beside it reading *Home of McBride Mustangs.*

"You brought me to your family ranch?"

"Yep."

"Why?"

"You'll see."

She managed not to scream. Just barely. They passed a sprawling two-story stone house with a long, wide porch, complete with rocking chairs, hanging baskets and pots of flowers. "Is that the house you grew up in?"

"It is. I'll show you later if you like, but for now, here we are." He pulled to a stop beside a large barn. The barn was a traditional red, with the white barn doors opened wide, flanking the opening.

"Did you bring me to see Jessie's mustangs? I've heard so much about them."

"Sure, you can see the mustangs. But I actually brought you out here to learn to ride. If you want to, that is."

Bella simply stared at him. Her voice, when she found it, came out in a squeak. "You...I get to...I'm going to ride a horse?"

"If you want to," he repeated.

"I'd love to." Bella had never thought she would ride a horse. She'd never known anyone with horses, or not well, anyway. "I've never been on a horse."

"I know. You told me once. One of Jessie's mares, one of the first horses she owned, is sweet as pie. Her name is Dulce."

"I saw the sign. Is she a mustang?"

"No, she's a cutting horse. But Jessie raises mustangs and also fosters them."

"Like people foster shelter pets?"

"Exactly. She tries to rehome them, but those she can't rehome stay here."

"How many horses does she have?"

"You know, I'm not sure. We'll have to ask her."

"I can't believe you did this for me."

"Every Texas girl should know how to ride."

Jessie came out just then leading a brown horse. It—she was a deep brown with a black mane and black feet. "Hi, Bella. This is Dulce. Say hello, Dulce."

The horse turned her head to look at Bella and whinnied. "Would you like to pet her?"

Don't be a chicken. Bella advanced gingerly. The horse was huge, at least in Bella's opinion. "I don't know what to do," she said, reaching Jessie's side. "I've never been this close to a horse before."

"Start by patting her neck. She's a sweetheart. Don't worry, she won't hurt you."

Bella patted her neck and when she didn't seem to mind, patted some more. "She's so soft."

"We take good care of her. Which reminds me, you'll see to her when y'all are finished, won't you, Graham? I'm getting ready for another mustang. He's due sometime today."

"Of course. Go away, Jessie. I can handle this."

"I wouldn't leave you if I thought you couldn't. See you later, Bella."

"I swear, she acts like I wasn't riding before she was even born," Graham grumbled as his sister left.

"I heard that," Jessie called back.

Graham took a good bit of time talking to her about horses and riding. He gave her a brush and showed her how to brush Dulce. He explained the parts of the saddle and which side of the horse to mount, and gave her tips about what she would do. Finally, he handed her a helmet and asked if she was ready.

"Why do I have to wear a helmet? People on TV don't."

"You have to wear it because you've never ridden before. Wearing a helmet is a lot more common now than it used to be, but not everyone wears one."

"Do you?"

"I plead the fifth."

"Meaning you don't. That doesn't seem fair."

"When you've been riding as long as I have, you can decide for yourself. Cheer up. I probably should but I can't make myself do it. Jessie wears one with the new horses. And she won't let anyone who's new to riding go without a helmet. So quit bitching and put it on if you want to ride."

"I'm not bitching," Bella protested.

Graham simply raised his eyebrows.

She frowned but she put on the helmet. Graham showed

her how to put her foot in the stirrup and swing herself into the saddle. She wiggled around, trying to settle herself.

"How do you feel?"

"Strange. Very strange." She looked down. "Good Lord, I'm awfully far from the ground."

Graham smiled and handed her the reins. "I'm sure it seems that way. But you'll be fine. I'm going to walk beside you, okay?"

"Whatever you say." They walked around the pen several times until Bella started to relax. "So when do we go faster?"

He glanced up at her with a curve of his lips. "We don't. Not for a while."

Eventually Graham let her trot. Not for long because apparently Dulce did not like to trot. Not to mention, it wasn't at all comfortable. So when Graham suggested that she drop back to a walk, she was happy.

When Graham decided she'd had enough he helped her get down—dismount, he called it—and then they began the process of cooling down the horse, giving her water, making sure she was dry, and brushing her. Finally, Graham put her in her stall, saying Jessie would decide whether to pasture her later.

"I had no earthly idea that you had to do all this stuff to take care of a horse."

"There's a lot more to it than just throwing on a saddle and riding."

"Amen to that."

"Come on and I'll take you to see the mustangs. They're out in one of the pastures."

"They're beautiful," Bella said when she saw the horses.

Leaning on the fence, Graham looked down at her and smiled. "Yes. When I see them like this, I can understand Jessie's obsession with them."

"Obsession?"

"Pretty much. It's much more than simply a business to her. She's involved with the Mustang Heritage Foundation and some mustang rescue groups as well."

"I admire that about her."

"So do I. But don't tell her I said that," he added with a wink.

Chapter Fifteen

JOEY DOUGLAS WAS one of Bella's favorite people. She was also one of her best friends. People often assumed the petite librarian was like the stereotype of a librarian. Mild, meek and unassuming. And in a way, she was. But beneath her work persona was, in Bella's opinion, a very different woman.

Bella had gotten to know Joey shortly after she came to Last Stand. Before she even opened the salon, in fact. She'd gone to the library to research a number of things, both online and in the library stacks. In fact, some of the things she wanted were available only in the room that held books and magazines that never left the library. Business tax records, commercial property taxes and a number of other things Bella felt she should know when opening a new business in a strange town.

Joey had been extremely helpful. And friendly. Before she knew it, they'd become good friends. Bella thought the friendship had really been cemented when Joey—a little shyly, which Bella had known by then wasn't typical—had asked Bella to put a bright crayon-red streak in her hair. And she wanted it permanent. What surprised Bella was that after that, more people hadn't tumbled onto the fact that Joey was anything but the quiet, shy, unassuming person they thought she was. Joey was, in fact, a bit of a rebel.

"My streak is growing out," Joey told Bella as she sat down in Bella's chair.

"Are you tired of it? Do you want me to take your color back to the original?"

"Heck, no! I need another dye job."

"Good, you had me worried." She left her station to go mix the color, returning shortly. "How is it going with you, Joey? I haven't seen much of you lately."

"No, and that's because you've been spending all your free time with that hunky doctor. And I've been dying to hear all about him. I mean, I've met him before, here at the library. But I don't know much about him. Other than what you told me early on."

"Graham's great."

Joey gave her a penetrating look. "So what's the problem?"

"Did I say there was a problem?"

"You didn't have to. Has Abby accepted him yet?"

She'd told both Joey and Delilah about Abby's sudden aversion. Bella separated out the preferred section of hair and began applying the color. "Yes, thank God. You should have seen Graham, Joey. Abby got stuck on top of the bookshelf and wouldn't or couldn't come down. Graham talked her down. It took him a while but he kept at it. After that, she even let him hold her and pet her."

"That's good. I know you said he was worried. So, if it's

not the cat, then what's the problem?"

Bella hesitated, trying to decide if she should talk to Joey truthfully about her growing feelings for Graham.

"Out with it," Joey said. "No one else will hear you. There's way too much noise in here today."

True, the shop was busy. Always a good thing. "You need a trim," she said, delaying the inevitable.

"Go for it. But I still want to know what's going on."

"I really like him, Joey." She leaned against her counter, waiting for Joey's color to process.

"You're dating the guy. You're supposed to like him."

"No, I mean I really, *really* like him. I like him too much."

Joey frowned. "Because he doesn't want to be serious? And you do?"

"Yes. No. Oh, crap, I don't know. I think I do, but he told me from the first he didn't want to get too involved. And I agreed with him."

"You changed your mind. Maybe Graham has, too."

"Maybe. I heard something at that fund-raiser he took me to that made me wonder...even if he changed his mind and decided he did want something more, it probably wouldn't work out." She told Joey what Fern had said and also that Graham used to date her.

"If she used to date him, that makes what she says a little suspect. She's probably just jealous and wanting to cause trouble."

"She's engaged to someone else. Why would she care?"

"Some women are just like that. I doubt Graham getting

that position hinges on who he's involved with. Besides that, it's not like there's something wrong with you. You're a successful business owner. You're involved in the town and you have a lot going for you."

"Thank you." She hesitated and then she blurted out, "I don't want to interfere with his career. It's too important to him."

"Why would you think that dating you would interfere with his career?"

"Why hasn't he told me about this chief of surgery position possibly being offered to him? It's not like we don't ever talk about his work."

"I don't know. Why don't you ask him?"

"Maybe I should."

"It sounds to me like you're letting Fern screw with your head. Stop that."

Bella laughed. "Yes, ma'am." If only it was that easy.

"ARE YOU TAKING Bella to the wedding this Saturday?" Turner asked Graham one evening as they both left the hospital.

Graham didn't know why but he saw his brothers a lot more entering and leaving the hospital than he did almost any other time.

"Dr. Prior's daughter's wedding, you mean?" Walter Prior was the chief of the surgery department and rumored to be retiring soon. No one knew who his replacement would be, but Graham knew he was on the list of possibilities. As was every other surgeon on staff. Graham had mixed emotions about being the chief. It sounded good and was supposed to be an honor, but he knew it involved a lot more paperwork than he already did. Which meant less time operating. And he wasn't anxious for that to happen.

As far as Graham knew, Dr. Prior had invited every doctor in the hospital as well as half the nurses, and most of the administrative staff. The reception promised to be a blowout.

"Yes, that one."

"I think I mentioned it to her a while back but I'll have to check."

"Good. It's about damn time you got over Cynthia."

Graham stopped walking at the elevators to the garage. "What's that supposed to mean? How does that have anything to do with my ex-wife?"

"You've gotten over Cynthia because of Bella. It's obvious things are getting serious between you two."

"You're imagining things."

Turner raised his eyebrows. "I haven't seen you take any other woman to a wedding. Or, for that matter, date anyone for longer than a month or so. You've been with Bella for at least a couple of months now, haven't you?"

Longer. Which he hadn't really thought about until now. "I've dated plenty of women for longer than a month."

"Yeah? Name one."

Damn it, he couldn't. "That's beside the point. Just because I'm taking Bella to a wedding doesn't mean we're serious." Did it?

"If you say so, Bro. FYI, Jessie thinks so too." He started to press the button on the elevator but Graham slapped a hand over it.

"Jessie? Why would—"

"You took Bella riding, remember?" Turner said when Graham broke off.

"Yes, but…she wanted to learn to ride. That was nothing."

"Not according to Jessie. She thinks you're totally gone over Bella. Now if you'll move your hand, I can get the elevator."

Graham argued with himself all the way home. Turner and Jessie were wrong. Yes, he liked Bella. He liked her a lot. But there was no way in hell he'd risk getting truly involved again. Once had been plenty. There were reasons. Good ones. His job was demanding and always would be. And even though Bella was okay with his hours now, and seemed to understand why his work was so important, that didn't mean she wouldn't change if they ever got serious. Besides, she was young and from what she'd said, was no more anxious to have a long-term relationship than he was.

But it really bugged him that Turner and Jessie thought he'd fallen for Bella. But that was just those two. Now if Spencer had noticed, he'd start to worry.

As he got into his car his phone rang. Speak of the devil: Spencer's ringtone. "Yeah."

"Hello to you too. Jessie wants to know if you're bringing Bella to poker Monday night."

Bring Bella to poker? Oh, hell, no. That was as good as a

proposal in his family. No one had tested it yet. Sure, they'd all brought friends on occasion, but no one brought casual dates to family poker night. "Why would I do that? And why doesn't Jessie ask me herself if she wants to know?"

"Well, duh. Because you're really into the woman. Obviously. And how do I know why Jessie does anything?" Spencer grumbled.

"I'll call Jessie. But no, I'm not bringing Bella to poker."

Don't panic. I'm not in love with Bella, so there's no reason to panic.

But you could be. That's why you're freaking out. She matters.

Of course she does. I don't date women who don't matter a damn to me. That doesn't mean I'm in love with any of them.

But Bella isn't like other women.

Graham turned on the radio really loudly, cutting his annoying subconscious off before he began listing all of Bella's amazing qualities. Take her to family poker night? Hell, no.

WHY IN THE hell did I think going to a wedding with Bella was a good idea?

Not that Bella had done anything wrong. No, she'd just looked unbelievably gorgeous when he picked her up. She wore a burgundy off-the-shoulder, low-cut sleeveless dress that cinched in at the waist and then flared, ending well above her knees. Very simple. Classy. Sexy.

Her long hair fell to her shoulders in waves and she'd worn it blonde. No colors. Just blonde. He'd have said something about it but he didn't want her to think he minded her colors. "You look beautiful."

"Thank you. I was a little worried. I wasn't sure what to wear."

"That's perfect." *Like you.*

Whoa, where had that come from?

The ceremony was just long enough to make him fidgety. It didn't help that he had flashbacks to his own wedding all those years ago. And to the disaster that followed. Or that his mind inexorably jumped to wondering what Bella would look like in a wedding dress.

She'd be beautiful, of course. Would she wear something traditional or something unusual? Would she color her hair or wear it blonde?

Damn it! What was wrong with him?

You're in love with Bella, that's what.

No, I'm not.

Oh, yeah. You're toast, buddy.

"Graham, is something wrong?" Bella asked as they walked to his car after the ceremony.

"No, why do you ask?"

"You've been awfully fidgety. And you haven't said much."

"I've been thinking about a case," he improvised.

"Oh, I hope it's nothing bad. Do you need to go check on your patient?"

Damn, couldn't she ever get irritated with him? "No, I

was thinking about an upcoming case."

"Okay. Do you want to go home instead of going to the reception?"

It wasn't Bella's fault he was acting squirrelly. "Of course not. I was just a little preoccupied."

She regarded him a little doubtfully but she let it go and started talking about how beautiful the ceremony had been. By the time they walked into the reception at the Carriage House, Graham was feeling even more twitchy. The bride and groom came in shortly after that and before long the dancing began. Which meant, thank God, that it was too loud to talk much.

"Do you want to dance?" Graham asked, fairly certain of her answer.

"No. I'm fine. Let's find a table."

Graham looked around for Turner but didn't see him, so they simply took a couple of empty seats at a table. "Still worried you can't dance?"

"No. But I know I don't do it well enough to go out there with everyone staring."

Too late, Graham realized that their table was directly in Fern Nixon's line of sight. At least they weren't trapped at the same table again.

"It's going to be awfully boring if you don't want to dance," he warned.

"I'll survive. Besides, I like looking at the people."

"Want me to get us a drink?"

"Yes, that would be good. Beer?"

"I'll be right back."

Graham ran into Turner on his way back. "I thought you came stag?" he asked his brother when he saw that Turner carried two drinks.

"I thought I would but I changed my mind. I brought Charlie."

They talked for a minute and the music stopped. Graham heard a woman's voice say, perfectly pitched for him to hear, "Bella Benson? Yes, he's dating her. Honestly, I don't know what he sees in that little nobody."

Fern Nixon. No surprise there. He didn't even think about it, he just reacted, leaving Turner staring at him.

"Hello, Fern," he said, walking the few steps to her and her friend. "Bella is a smart, successful, compassionate, beautiful woman. And those are only some of the things I see in her."

Her mouth literally fell open. "Graham, I didn't realize you were standing there."

He raised an eyebrow. "Didn't you?"

Fern stared at him in feigned astonishment. "Why, Graham, you sound like you're in love with the girl. You *can't* be serious."

He was a millimeter away from saying, "You're damn right I'm in love with Bella." But he managed not to say it. Instead he said, "Serious as a heart attack." He turned his back on her and started to go to Bella but Turner was in his way.

"Really? Serious as a heart attack?" Turner said.

Graham shrugged bad-temperedly. "There were a lot worse things I could have said to her. Much worse."

"Don't you think you overreacted just a tad?"

"No. Get out of the way. The beer's going to be warm by the time I get back to Bella."

"You're in love with her."

"No, I'm not."

"Have it your way, Bro. But it sure looks that way from where I'm standing."

Fortunately, his brother left, removing the temptation to slug him.

"What in the world is wrong, Graham?" Bella asked when he handed her the beer.

"Nothing."

"Was that Fern you were talking to? What did she say that pissed you off?"

"Nothing. She's just annoying."

She tilted her head as if trying to figure out something. "She said something ugly about me, didn't she?"

"Why would you think that?"

"Just a hunch. She doesn't like me."

"Count yourself lucky, then. She's not worth ten seconds of your time. Now, can we forget her?"

Bella studied him for a minute. He didn't think she was going to let it go but she shrugged and said, "Sure."

"Come on, let's dance. It's a slow one. We can just stand there and sway."

"I'd rather go home and do that."

He smiled at her. "Works for me. Definitely works for me."

Chapter Sixteen

B ELLA AND GRAHAM didn't talk much on the way home. He wasn't fidgety like he'd been but he seemed to be...well, brooding was the word she'd use to describe him. He'd said he was worried about a case, though, so maybe that was all it was.

She opened the door to her apartment and Abby came out immediately to greet them. To greet Graham, she thought with a smile. "You know, I could be jealous of you."

Graham had reached down to run his hand along Abby's spine but he looked up at that. "What can I say? Ladies like me."

She laughed but he was absolutely right. Women did like him. She watched him take off his suit coat and drape it over a dining room chair. She kicked off her shoes and asked, "Do you want something to drink? Water? Something else?" She knew he didn't want alcohol since he'd had beer at the reception and she'd never seen him drink more than a couple of beers, and usually only one.

"No, but I'll tell you what I do want." He walked over to her, swung her up in his arms and headed for the bedroom. "You."

He kissed her, his tongue seeking hers, teasing and retreating until they were both breathing heavily. He set her down beside the bed, Bella making sure she rubbed against him as he did so. She started to take off her dress, but Graham turned her around and unzipped her, kissing along her spine as he did. He undressed her slowly, kissing the skin he bared as he did so. First her neck, then her back, then sliding the dress down over her breasts and pressing his lips along the lace of her bra. He paused to take one of her nipples into his mouth, suckling it through the sheer fabric of her bra. She groaned and sank her hands into his hair. He unhooked her bra and let it fall, leaving her wearing only her thong.

"Take this off," she said, her fingers at his shirt buttons. He let her unbutton it, then shrugged it off and tossed it aside.

He sat on the bed and took off his shoes and socks, but his eyes never left her, gazing at her hungrily. The way he looked at her made her hot. And wet. Just thinking about what was ahead of her made her ache between her thighs. He reached for her hand, bringing her to stand between his legs. His gaze locked with hers, he caressed her breasts, plucked at her nipples until they were hard and aching. Then he took one in his mouth and sucked on it strongly. She'd had no idea her breasts were that sensitive. He moved to the other breast, taking long pulls that made her shudder, made her want.

Bella put her arms around his neck and kissed his mouth, whispered, "I want you."

He stood and got rid of his pants and boxers while she lay on the bed on her back, watching him. In the moonlight, she saw him smile and it seemed to take him even longer to rid himself of his clothes.

"Devil," she said.

His grin flashed and then he was naked, on the bed beside her. He made love to her slowly, sensuously. With his hands touching everywhere. With his lips taking the place of his hands. And when he finally slipped inside her and she wrapped her legs tight around him, he rode her slowly at first and finally, finally faster and faster until she cried out his name as she came. He followed, exploding inside her with her name on his lips.

She loved him. So much. Was it too much to hope that he loved her too?

THE LAST THING Graham wanted to do was go to family poker night. But if he didn't go, he'd never hear the end of it. He might as well suck it up and go. Still, after his little chat with Spencer, he knew they'd all want to know why he didn't bring Bella. And what could he say?

Because he liked her too much? Because he was falling in love with her? Because he'd already fallen in love with her? And taking her to poker would sound the death knell on his vow to remain single. Uninvolved. Move on easily.

So he called her. "Hey, I can't see you tonight. I'm going to be tied up with family crap."

"Okay, I've got some paperwork I need to do anyway," Bella said.

Perversely, it irritated him that she was so accepting. "I know you had plans for us but I forgot."

"It's fine, Graham. It wasn't anything major."

And she meant it. She was perfectly fine with whatever he needed to do. There wasn't a clingy bone in her body. Damn it.

Consequently, Graham wasn't in the best of moods when he got to his parents' house that night. The entire family was there tonight. His mom made her famous chili, which was one of his favorite meals. Maybe tonight wouldn't be so bad after all, he thought as he dug in.

"Graham, I thought you'd bring Bella tonight," his mother said. "Did she have other plans?"

"No. I didn't ask her. Besides, why would I bring her? I never bring anyone I'm dating."

"Bella isn't just some woman you're dating," Jessie said.

"What's that supposed to mean?"

"Oh, honey," his smart-ass baby sister said. "The big L. Turner told us what happened at Lucinda Prior's wedding."

He glared at his brother. "Nothing happened."

"Come on, Graham," Turner said. "You about had a shit fit when Fern Nixon dissed Bella."

"I was irritated. That's all."

"You totally overreacted."

"So? She's an obnoxious bitch. And I didn't overreact." Oh, hell yes, he had overreacted big-time.

"Fern Nixon?" Graham's dad said, entering the conversation for the first time. "Sounds like she's taken after her mother, Annette." He turned to his wife. "I remember when you lit into Annette, Rita. You know, when she—"

"Yes, but we don't need to talk about that," Rita said hastily. "Now where were we?"

"We were talking about Graham and how he's finally taken the fall," Spencer said. "That's why we thought you'd bring Bella," he said to Graham.

"Damn it, I haven't 'taken the fall.' I'm not in love with Bella. We're dating. That's all. It's not a big deal."

All three of his siblings started laughing. His parents didn't but he could tell they were struggling not to.

"Whose turn is it to clean up?" Rita asked. "Isn't it you, Graham?"

It wasn't but he took the out gratefully. He stacked his plates and carried them to the kitchen. Everyone brought their dishes in and Turner, Spencer, and Jessie finished clearing the table while Graham rinsed off everything that would fit in the dishwasher and hand washed the rest. His mother came in and started drying. "You don't need to do that," Graham said. "You cooked—you don't clean or dry dishes."

"I told everyone to go on and set up the game so I could talk to you."

"Mom, I love you but I don't want to talk about Bella anymore."

"Yes, that's obvious. So we'll talk about what's really bothering you." Graham said nothing, knowing his mother would get her point across no matter what he said. "Cynthia."

"Cynthia? Good God, Mom, we've been divorced for years. I haven't thought of her since—" He broke off, remembering that he'd thought of his ex not two days ago. "She's not a problem."

"Not Cynthia herself, but how she treated you. How much she hurt you."

"It wasn't fun at the time but I'm long over it."

"Are you? Then why haven't you had a serious girlfriend in more than ten years? Until Bella, that is."

He gritted his teeth. Ignoring her comment about Bella, he said, "You of all people should know what it's like being married to a doctor. A conscientious one, anyway."

"Of course I do. And I'll be the first to admit it's hard sometimes. But marriage is hard at times, period. Some women aren't cut out to be a doctor's wife. Or a cop's, a firefighter's, a soldier's. But if you love them, you make it work. Cynthia was entirely too self-involved. Of course your marriage fell apart. But all women aren't like that. It doesn't sound as if Bella is."

"I'm not in love with Bella," he repeated.

"All right. You can tell me and the rest of the family whatever you want, but do yourself a favor. Don't lie to yourself. It never works out well." She laid down her towel. "Don't be long. They'll have started already."

Tempted to throw something, he watched his mother leave the room. He wasn't lying to himself. He knew, had known for weeks, that he was falling in love with Bella. Turner was right. He'd overreacted to something stupid and bitchy Fern had said. If he hadn't been in love with Bella, he'd have been annoyed, yes. But he'd probably have ignored the comments.

Great, he thought in disgust. He loved her. Did she love him? He knew she cared about him, but she'd never seemed too interested in taking the relationship further. And even if she did love him, he still couldn't be sure she wouldn't change if they married. Cynthia had. Would Bella? Was he willing to risk having his heart ripped out?

Even if he was willing to risk that neither of them would change with marriage, there were other considerations. He knew all too well how precarious life was. Just last week, he'd sent one of his patients and his wife to Houston to see if he was a candidate for a heart transplant. It had been painfully clear the couple was madly in love. Worse, they were young and thought they'd have their whole lives ahead of them. Until Graham had given them the news that without a transplant he would die. And there was no guarantee that he would get one.

SOMETHING WAS DEFINITELY going on with Graham. He hadn't been himself since that wedding they had gone to together. Bella still thought that Fern had been saying catty things about her. It didn't particularly bother Bella, but clearly it had irked Graham. No, she thought it was the wedding... Maybe the wedding had brought back memories of his ex-wife. And what if those memories hadn't been all bad?

But if that was it, how could he have made love to her so tenderly afterward? So sweetly? So...lovingly. Something had shifted in their relationship that night. They'd gone from simply having a good time together to something else. Something more.

They. The two of them. Not just her.

She loved Graham. She'd known it for weeks now, even if she hadn't admitted it to herself until the night of the wedding. She was 100 percent madly in love with Graham McBride. How in the hell had that happened? And what was she going to do about it? Was it completely foolish to hope that he felt the same? Was she reading too much into what had happened over the weekend?

She hadn't seen him since Monday morning. He'd stayed Saturday night, Sunday and Sunday night but since then he'd canceled on her Monday to do something with his family, and the rest of the week, he had several excuses— including work—for why they couldn't get together. It was Saturday night before she saw him again.

Bella had offered to cook but he'd said he had some things to do and for her to eat without him. On her way home from the salon, she picked up a pizza. When she got home, she sat down with a beer, pizza, and the recorded shows she'd missed all week. Perfect, except she wished Graham was there.

By the time Graham showed up, Bella had changed into her pajamas—a T-shirt and flannel pajama pants. She could tell immediately that something was wrong. For one thing, he didn't kiss her hello. She couldn't remember the last time that had happened.

"Did something bad happen at work?" she asked when she let him in. "You seem upset."

"It's not work." He didn't sit but Abby came over and rubbed against his legs until he petted her.

"I hope it's not your family."

"They're fine." He still didn't sit down but paced, glancing at her occasionally as if he had something to say but didn't know how to say it.

Bella started to get a bad feeling. She sat on the couch and waited for him to speak. "Just spit it out," she finally said.

He stopped pacing, but stood some distance away. "I think we need some time apart."

She felt like he'd gut-punched her. "Why?"

"This—you and me—" he motioned between them "—we're getting too serious. I need space. I need some time alone. So do you."

"Bullshit. Don't tell me what I need."

"All right. Fine. *I* need some space."

"Space. Is that code for you're breaking up with me?"

He scrubbed a hand over his face. "I'm not trying to hurt you, Bella. I just think it would be better for us to call it quits now. Before we become any more involved."

And there it was. "I don't remember asking you to live with me. Or, God forbid, marry me."

"I didn't say you had. But you can't deny we've been together a lot over the last few months. Or that we've grown close. Closer than either of us intended."

No, she couldn't deny it. She couldn't deny that she'd agreed that she didn't want to get serious either. That had just happened. For her, anyway. Graham had never said he was in love with her. It was her bad luck she'd fallen for him. What a stupid thing to do. *Suck it up, Bella.*

"All right." She stood and walked to the door. "You can go now."

"That's all you're going to say? All right? You can go now?"

"What more is there to say?"

"I thought you might—"

"What? Beg you not to break up with me? Cry? Wail? Gnash my teeth?" She gave him a mocking smile. "Sorry, Graham. Not my style. Now if you'll excuse me." She opened the door and stood there waiting patiently for him to walk through it.

He stopped in the middle of the doorway. "Bella, I didn't want to hurt you."

"Yes, you said that before. Goodbye, Graham." He left and she shut the door behind him. It took a supreme effort of will not to slam it. For a moment, she stood there stunned. She walked over to the couch and clicked on the TV. Abby jumped up beside her, bumped her hand until she put it on the cat's back and stroked her.

"What am I going to do?" she whispered to Abby. And then, the tears flowed.

Chapter Seventeen

OKAY, HE'D DONE it. He'd broken up with Bella. He knew it was for the best. They—no, *he*—was getting too involved. He still didn't believe he could make a marriage work. The way they were going, he was only going to fall more deeply in love with her. And when it inevitably ended, and it would, both of them would suffer even more. So he ended it now. Better for both of them that way.

He hated that he'd hurt Bella. She'd masked her feelings, beyond commenting that she hadn't asked him to live with her or marry her, but he knew the breakup had come out of the blue to her. Good God, he'd been on the verge of telling her he loved her Saturday night. He wouldn't be a bit surprised if she hadn't known that, or at the least, suspected it.

Bella was better off without him. She needed someone closer to her own age, someone who could devote the time to her that she deserved.

This is all pure bullshit. You broke up with her because you fell in love with her and that freaked you out. Stop trying to make yourself out as anything other than a selfish prick.

Which was, undoubtedly, true. Regardless, it was done

now so he needed to get on with his life.

His phone rang with Jessie's ringtone. It was still early but his sister got up early anyway to tend to the horses. "Hi, Jessie."

"Hi. Listen, I wondered when you wanted to bring Bella out again to ride. Sometime this week? Or are you going to wait—"

"I won't be bringing her out there."

"What? Why? She liked riding. I know she did."

He really hadn't wanted to announce the breakup to his family yet, but there was no help for it now. "We broke up."

"What? You did what?"

"We broke up," he repeated. "And if you don't mind, I don't want to talk about it."

"Well, I do mind. What happened, Graham? You two were so good together. Did she break it off?"

"No. I did."

"What?" she yelled.

He yanked the phone away from his ear. When he was certain she was through yelling he said, "Don't screech."

"What is wrong with you?" she asked but at least she'd lowered her voice.

"It wasn't working. That's all I'm going to say."

"Fine, I can't make you talk, but I can sure as hell tell you what I think. You're an idiot to let her go."

"Thanks for the support."

"Why would I support you doing something so stupid?"

"Let it go, Jessie."

"Graham, don't do this," she pleaded. "You've been so

happy. For the first time since your divorce, I thought you'd finally found the right woman."

He closed his eyes. "It's too late. I've already done it."

Fortunately, he was busy operating most of the day so his mind was on his work rather than a certain beautiful blonde. He ran into Spencer as he was leaving the hospital.

"Hey, I'm off for the next few days," his brother said. "Let's go get a beer at the Saloon."

He tried to get out of it but Spencer was determined, so he gave in. When Spencer wanted something, he didn't give up until he got it. All of his family was like that. He supposed he was too.

They found a booth in the back, which suited Graham just fine. Spencer went off to get them a couple of beers. He came back with them shortly. "Here's to the single life. Again."

Graham took a hefty drink of beer before speaking. "You talked to Jessie."

"Yeah, she called at the butt-crack of dawn, right after she hung up with you. She wants me to get on your case but I told her that was not happening."

"I appreciate that but why?"

"Why aren't I on your case? Isn't that obvious?" He took a swig of his beer.

"Not to me."

"Don't be stupid, Bro. Now I'm free to ask her out myself."

Graham choked on his beer. "What?" he roared.

"Hey, you don't want her. She's a beautiful woman.

There wasn't any point thinking about it when you two were dating but now that you've cut her loose, that makes her fair game."

"The hell she is."

"Sorry to point this out but you no longer have a say in the matter. I wouldn't poach, especially not on my brother, but you broke up with her. Didn't you?"

"Damn it, yes. But that doesn't give you free rein to ask her out."

"Why not?"

Spencer had him there. He could think of no reasonable answer, but there were a whole lot of unreasonable ones. His brother drank his beer, seemingly not a bit concerned about Graham's opinion.

The silence lengthened. Spencer finally broke it. "Could it be because you're in love with her?"

"Go to hell."

"Not an answer."

"Damn you. Yes."

"That's what I thought. So why did you break up with her?"

"*Because* I'm in love with her."

"You realize that makes no sense, right?"

Graham scrubbed a hand over his face, then drank some of his beer. "I can't go through it again, Spencer."

"Go through what? Being in love?"

"Being in love. Having it fall apart again. It about killed me when Cynthia and I divorced and I didn't feel half for her of what I feel for Bella. If I'm this crazy about her now, what's it going to be like later? When we've both invested more time, fallen more in love, and we find out it just won't work."

"Why won't it work?"

He put his hands to his temples, then dropped them to look at his brother. "You're a paramedic and a firefighter. You know how quickly you can lose people. You've seen what happens to those who are left behind."

"And?"

What could he say? He didn't want that pain. The pain of losing the love of his life.

"Let me get this straight. You're afraid you're going to lose her so you called it off now rather than later?"

"It sounds stupid when you put it that way."

"That's because it is stupid. What kind of a dumbass are you? That's like saying you're never going to have a pet because they don't live as long as you do. You're denying yourself the joy of what you have now because of a *possibility* of pain later. If I had a woman like Bella, you can bet your ass I'd be holding on with both hands. Not, for God's sake, breaking up with her."

Graham started to speak but Spencer held up a hand. "I'm not finished. On top of that, it's not solely your decision to make. Did you even talk to her about what's bothering you?"

"It's not that simple." He sighed and drained his beer.

"So you didn't. You just what, walked in and said, 'Hey, babe, we're done'?"

Graham didn't answer. But Spencer wasn't done.

"Is Bella in love with you?"

"I don't know. She's never said, but we were getting close. Too close."

Spencer stared at him. "I've known you my whole life and I've never known you to be a chickenshit. Until now."

BY THE TIME she went back to work on Tuesday, Bella thought she had her shit together. She'd spent Sunday and Monday at home indulging herself in movies and chocolate, looking like crap, playing with Abby. And crying, but only at the movies, she assured herself. Not over Graham. No, if he didn't want her, she sure as hell didn't want him.

I wish.

The test, she knew, was how she handled herself when Delilah came in this morning. She hadn't told anyone that she and Graham had broken up. In fact, she hadn't left the house. She'd had pizza delivered and otherwise scrounged around for food. But it was time to face the world again. She'd thrown her pity party and now she was done with it.

So she plastered a smile on her face and faked it like it was an ordinary day. Delilah came in talking, thank God. Bella pretended she was listening but she honestly had no idea what her friend had said.

"Bella? What's wrong?"

"What?"

"What's wrong? You haven't heard a word I've said."

"Of course I did."

"Really? Then what do you think about the new delicatessen going in a few doors down from you?"

"I think it's a great idea. We can always use more restaurants."

"I didn't say anything about a new deli. I made it up. So what's up with you?"

"Nothing. I'm just a little distracted."

"Bullshit." Delilah peered closely at her in the mirror. "You've been crying. A lot. Your eyes are swollen."

Damn Delilah's sharp eyes. "I have allergies," she said, sniffing for emphasis.

"Since when?"

Bella felt tears threaten. "Can we not do this here? Please?"

Delilah opened her mouth, then shut it. "Okay. But can we talk later? After work? I'm off tonight."

Bella closed her eyes, willing herself not to cry. "All right. Come over to my apartment about six."

"Do you want to get a bite to eat?"

"Bring some burgers. Not pizza." God knows she'd had enough pizza in the last few days to sink a battleship. "I have beer. And while you're at it, bring some ice cream."

"See you then."

Somehow, she made it through the rest of the day. By the time Delilah got there she had changed into ancient jeans, one of her favorite T-shirts and piled her hair on top of her head, fastening it with a big clip. They went to the kitchen. Delilah parceled out the burgers and fries and after putting away the ice cream, Bella set out paper plates, paper towels for napkins, ketchup and a couple of beers.

"Thanks for bringing the food. I didn't feel like going out."

"Let's eat and then you can tell me what's going on." Delilah then kept up a running commentary about town gossip. Bella managed to eat some of her food even though she wasn't hungry. They finished eating, cleaned up and then went into the den, carrying what was left of their beers.

"Are you ready for ice cream?" Bella asked.

Abby jumped up on the couch beside Delilah, demanding attention. Delilah was one of her favorite people. Like Graham had become, she thought morosely.

"We'll get to the ice cream later. I'm pretty sure I know what happened," Delilah said.

"That obvious, huh?"

"Yes. First of all you never cry and you've clearly been crying or struggling not to cry for days. Your place is a mess. I've never seen it look like this. And you haven't mentioned Graham, not even once. You two broke up, didn't you?"

"He broke up with me. He needed 'space,'" she said making air quotes. "He was afraid we were getting *too close*."

"Were you?"

"I was. Obviously, he wasn't. Not if he could walk away without a backward glance."

"Do you know what precipitated it?"

"No. Not really." She thought about that. Again. "He'd been a little different before the Prior wedding. Kind of…twitchy. I asked him about it but he blew me off. Said it was nothing. Then at the wedding, he and Fern Nixon had some kind of run-in. I think she said something ugly about me."

"She did. From what I heard, Fern said something catty and Graham lost it big-time."

"Lost it how?"

"She said something about she couldn't imagine what he saw in you. Graham totally overreacted and yelled at her that you were smart and beautiful and so on and so forth. Fern was left with her mouth hanging open. Which sounds to me like he is totally in love with you."

"Then why in the hell did he break up with me? What did it? We were fine. We were good. But after he left Monday morning, I didn't talk to him for days except when he canceled on me. He said he had a family thing."

"And the next time you saw him was when he broke up with you?"

Bella nodded. "Yes."

"What did you say?"

"I said all right and kicked his ass out of my apartment."

"Good for you."

"Yay me," Bella said sarcastically. "There's just one problem."

"Which is?"

"I'm still in love with him."

THURSDAY BELLA HAD an hour break in the morning so she indulged herself and went to Char-Pie, the pie shop owned by Charlotte—Charlie—Stockton and her sister, Audrey. If anyone deserved a slice of lemon meringue pie, she decided, it was her. As usual it was crowded but they were always quick. Bella took her pie to one of the small tables and sat down to enjoy it.

Damn it! Wouldn't you know it. Fern Nixon sat at the table next to her. One of the two people in town she really didn't want to see, the other being Graham. Luckily, Fern only nodded at her so she didn't have to talk.

Naturally, the next person to enter the shop was Graham himself. She tried to ignore him, wishing he'd take his pie and go the hell away. Watching him surreptitiously, she saw he had his pie in a to-go container and breathed a sigh of relief. Too soon. He and his pie walked over to her.

"Hi, Bella. How are you?"

Just dandy. Now go away. "Good. And you?" She thought he looked a little ragged but that was probably either wishful thinking or a rough night on call.

"I'm uh, good." He looked like he wanted to say more but she didn't give him an opening.

"Great," she said.

"Great," he said.

He stood there for a moment, looking at her. She stared right back. Wishing she could hate him or at least be indifferent to him.

"Good to see you," he finally said, and left.

Good to see you, my ass. She hated that she wanted to cry. Just seeing him had ruined her day. And it was going to get worse. There was no way to avoid him in a town the size of

Last Stand. She'd run into him everywhere, unless she stayed in her house or her salon. Unfortunately, that wasn't feasible.

"Hello, Bella," Fern said. "May I sit with you a moment?"

Short of saying no or hell, no, which would only generate a lot of talk, she had no response, so she merely nodded.

Fern settled herself in the other chair and leaned forward. "I couldn't help noticing that little scene between you and Graham. Is everything all right?" she asked with fake concern.

What was the point in lying? Everyone would know soon enough. "No. We broke up."

"Oh, I'm so sorry."

I bet.

"I'm not really surprised, though. After all," she said with a tinkly laugh, "you're hardly his type."

She couldn't help it. She bit. "And what would his type be?"

"Well, you know," Fern said airily. "Someone with education and social standing. A woman of breeding. Or even a professional, such as another doctor. Or a lawyer. But you know, Graham is pretty particular. I'm surprised the two of you lasted as long as you did. He must have finally realized you'd only hold him back in his career. Or he just grew tired of you."

Bella considered her options. She could tell her to take a hike. Better yet, she could smash her pie into Fern's snarky smiling face. But she was above that sort of thing. Regretfully. She stared at Fern for a long moment. At her carefully styled, rather brassy hair color.

"You know, I could fix that hair color for you," she said, loud enough for most of the people in the shop to hear. Especially since the noise had died down and everyone was listening.

Fern goggled, then sputtered. "You, you—"

"I'll be happy to fix it. Take that brassiness right out. I've got a way with color. Ask anyone. Just make an appointment."

She picked up her plate and carried it to the bucket for dirty dishes, and left the shop with her head held high.

Graham breaking up with her really didn't make sense. Unless Fern was right and Graham was afraid she'd hold him back. He still hadn't mentioned anything about being offered the soon-to-be-vacant chief of surgery position. But why would he, if he intended to break up with her before that happened?

Chapter Eighteen

I T HAD BEEN two weeks since he'd called off things with Bella. Graham knew he wasn't totally over her, but at least he felt like he had a handle on things now. Of course, he hadn't actually seen her or spoken to her since running into her in the pie shop, nearly two weeks ago now. That had been awkward, to say the least. Still, he felt like he was almost back to normal. Not enough to want to go out with anyone, however. Maybe he'd swear off women for a while.

His mother—his mother, of all people—had other plans. An old friend of hers and her daughter were in town and Rita had volunteered him to take the daughter—Darla Henderson—to dinner at Dragonfly, Delilah Corbyn's restaurant on the river. He had no idea why Rita was so determined that he do so, but she was.

Fortunately, Darla was a very pretty, very nice woman a few years younger than him, who he had absolutely nothing in common with other than they were both divorced. Darla was a high-powered attorney from Dallas. He didn't think she was enjoying herself any more than he was. But they were both making the best of it. Then Bella walked in.

Her hair looked like fire. She'd colored it in reds, oranges and golds, the exact colors of a fire. It fell past her shoulders in long, smooth waves. She had on some kind of curve-hugging, short cocktail dress that matched the color of her hair. She wore heels, black barely there spike heels and she looked absolutely stunning.

He finally noticed she'd come in with a man who looked familiar but he couldn't place him at first. Then he remembered. This was Rex, the man she'd claimed was just a friend. Rex was a big guy, with wide shoulders and looked like he either spent a lot of time pumping iron or more likely, given his tan, working outside. He had a depressing feeling that women would consider the man good-looking. Bella seemed totally at ease with him. Graham couldn't tell whether that was a good or a bad thing.

Why was he surprised that she was dating? There was absolutely no reason she shouldn't date whoever she wanted. No reason, except he couldn't stand seeing her with another man. Even one she'd claimed was only a friend. Maybe she'd changed her mind after they broke up.

Bella was laughing at something Rex said when he caught her eye. She looked right at him, gave a little wave, then turned back to her date. As if Graham was someone she barely knew.

"Graham, is there something wrong?" Darla asked him.

He yanked his attention away from Bella and back to his date. "Not at all. How is your fish?"

"Delicious. How is yours?"

"Great."

Before the silence grew too much longer or more awkward, Darla asked him a question. "I was a bit surprised when I learned you were a cardiothoracic surgeon. I would have thought you needed to practice at a bigger hospital with that sort of specialty."

"Typically that's true. But in the late nineties our hospital was given a very generous gift to modernize and expand. Now we service a large area, drawing patients from all over the Hill Country."

"Oh, I see. So you obviously like living in a small town."

"I do." He glanced at Bella again. "Most of the time." His gaze narrowed as he watched Bella's date take her hand and hold it. She didn't appear to mind.

Darla glanced over her shoulder in the direction of Bella's table. "Ah. So that's it."

"Pardon me?"

"I couldn't figure out what in the world you kept staring at. Your ex, I take it?"

He shrugged, not bothering to deny it. "Not my ex-wife. My ex-girlfriend."

"I'd say I'd take an Uber home so you can go make up with her, but I doubt Last Stand has any, do they?"

"No. And I wouldn't have you do that anyway. I'm sorry, that was unforgivably rude of me."

"No offense taken. You know, Graham, it's pretty obvious you're not over this woman."

He drank some of his beer. "I'm not. I thought I was, but I was wrong."

"She's very pretty. Unusual. Why don't you take me back to the hotel and see if you can make up with her?"

"Thanks, but I don't ditch my dates." Besides, Bella was here with a date and didn't look at all like she wanted to be rescued.

Darla laughed. "I'm sure we both know that our mothers cooked up this *date*. I promise, I won't take offense."

"Nope. You haven't even had dessert yet. Let's order some and I promise—"

His phone rang. The hospital's ringtone. "Sorry, I have to take this. It's the hospital." He answered as he got up and walked out of the dining room. "Dr. McBride."

Luckily, it was one of the hospitalists asking about a patient and not a call to come in. He took care of it and went back to Darla, deliberately not looking at Bella. Which took more willpower than he'd expected.

"Now, where were we?" he asked as he sat down. "About to order dessert, weren't we?"

"Yes, but would you mind terribly if I took mine back to the hotel? I'm full right now but I know I'll want some later."

"Of course." He signaled the waiter, asked for the dessert to go and the check. A short time later he and Darla left. On the way out, he nodded at Bella but didn't stop to talk. He figured neither of them really wanted that. Besides, damn it, her date was holding her hand again.

No matter that he told himself that seeing her hold hands with this Rex guy meant absolutely nothing, he wondered if it did mean more. He couldn't stop the thought of Bella in another man's arms. Of another man holding her, kissing her, caressing her, making love to her... And the corresponding thought that he wanted to kill any man who touched her.

Jealousy was a bitch. And he only had himself to blame.

🙞

"THANK YOU FOR tonight. Dinner was wonderful," Bella said when they left the restaurant.

Rex shot her an enigmatic glance but didn't say anything.

In fact, the only thing he did say when they reached her apartment complex was, "I need to talk to you. Can I come in?"

"Of course," she said, even though she didn't feel like company. Honestly, she should have refused to go at all but after he apologized for being a jerk the last time she'd seen him, she'd felt obligated to say yes. But she felt guilty because she knew she hadn't been paying attention to Rex as she should have. She'd been too busy obsessing over Graham. She suspected Rex knew it too.

Abby greeted them when they came in. Her cat liked Rex. Always had. He petted her, but absentmindedly. "What was it you wanted to talk to me about, Rex?" Bella asked him.

"You're still in love with McBride, aren't you?"

Oh, yeah, he knew it. "We broke up. I told you that."

"Yes, that's what you said but you're obviously still hung up on him."

"It doesn't matter. He's moved on. He was there with a

date."

"So were you," Rex said, a little acerbically.

"I'm sorry. I told you I wouldn't be good company."

"Never mind that. Can we sit down?"

"Of course." She sat on the couch and he sat beside her. He took her hands in his and held them before speaking. He'd held her hand several times tonight. Something he didn't ordinarily do.

"We've talked about this before, but I have a reason for bringing it up again. I've been in love with you since the day we met."

She started to speak but he hushed her. "Let me talk. Please. You told me from the first that you wanted to be friends and I accepted that. I hoped you'd change your mind and some day you'd feel the same about me as I do about you. But you never have."

"I'm sorry, Rex. I don't want to hurt you." She'd wondered why she only felt friendship for him. He was a good guy. He'd always treated her well. He had a good job working in construction. They had a lot of interests in common. He was funny, kind and good-looking but she'd never felt the intense attraction to him that she'd felt with Graham from the first.

"You've been very honest from the beginning. Then you started dating McBride and I knew that was it for you. Don't bother to deny it."

"I won't. I wish it wasn't true."

"When you two broke up I thought that finally there might be a chance for us."

"Is that what tonight was about?"

He gave her a rueful smile. "Yeah. And I got my answer." He released her hands.

"Rex, I really do care about you—"

He held up a hand. "I know. But not the way I want you to. So, I wanted to tell you I'm moving."

"Moving? Away from Last Stand? Because of me?" Now she really felt guilty.

"Partly. But mostly because it's time for me to move on. I've got some good jobs lined up in Austin. And there's nothing keeping me here."

"But you love it here in Last Stand."

"No." He shook his head. "*You* love it here. To me it's just been another place to work. If I hadn't met you, I'd have moved quite a while ago."

"I—I don't know what to say."

"There's nothing to say." He got up, took her hand and pulled her up too. "You have my phone number. You know you can call if you need me."

"When are you going?"

"Next week."

"I wish you weren't leaving."

"It's past time I was." He took her in his arms and murmured, "Just once." And then he kissed her.

A real kiss. Not the friendly, quick touch of the lips he'd given her from time to time. But a kiss like he hadn't attempted since she'd told him she just wanted to be friends. A masterful kiss with lips and tongue and heat, one which asked for entry and demanded response. She kissed him back, admitting it was a good, even a great kiss. But for her, there was no heart behind it. Because her foolish heart belonged to Graham.

He released her. "Goodbye, Bella. Take care of yourself."

She was an idiot. She couldn't love the man who loved and wanted her. She loved the one who didn't want her. The man who'd broken her heart.

FOR THE NEXT three days Graham was consumed with work. Not only was he taking his own call, but he was filling in for another doctor whose wife just had a baby. It was a good thing that while he was actually working, he had no time to think about Bella and worse, worry that he'd made a terrible mistake in breaking up with her.

But there was always some down time. And inevitably he thought of Bella then. Wondered if she was seeing Rex. Wondered if they'd made the change from friends to lovers. Drove himself insane thinking of Bella with anyone else but him.

When he finally got off work he went home and crashed for sixteen hours. And woke up dreaming of Bella. Aching for her. Wanting her...so damn badly. Why had he ever thought letting her go was the right thing to do?

What the hell was he doing? Besides making himself miserable. He thought about what Spencer had said. *It's not solely your decision to make. Bella deserves the chance to say yes or no.* And then, in his usual straightforward manner, his brother told him he was a chickenshit.

Spencer was right. He was a chickenshit. First he'd let the past color what he had with Bella, thinking she could turn out to be like Cynthia, when he should have known Bella was a completely different person. And later, when he'd fallen absolutely, totally, completely in love with Bella, he let fear of a possibility ruin the future he could have with Bella. And instead of telling her he loved her and asking her to marry him, he'd broken up with her.

What a dumbass.

He wanted her back. Now he had to figure out how to accomplish that.

Unless…could she have changed her mind about Rex? In less than three weeks?

It was possible. Maybe even…likely.

Graham knew Bella still cared about him. But she'd never said she loved him. Because she didn't? Or because she didn't want to open up to him when he hadn't admitted his own feelings for her?

First things first. He needed to see Bella. Talk to her in person. Gauge how angry and/or hurt she still was. Apologize for being a fool. Ask her if they could try again.

He texted her.

CAN I COME SEE YOU?

It took a long time for her to answer. Belatedly, he realized it was the Fourth of July. Bella had probably gone to the rodeo or one of the gazillion other activities that happened in Last Stand on the fourth. He forced himself not to check his phone more than once an hour. The damn thing would chime when he got a text. Checking it served no purpose other than to drive him crazy. Finally, he heard a chime and snatched up the phone.

> WHY?
>
> I NEED TO SEE YOU. TALK TO YOU IN PERSON.
>
> WHY?
>
> IT'S NOT SOMETHING I CAN PUT IN A TEXT. I REALLY NEED TO SEE YOU IN PERSON. PLEASE?

Another long pause. So long he wondered if she would answer.

> I'LL THINK ABOUT IT AND LET YOU KNOW.

Graham stared at the screen. She'd think about it? What the hell?

Chapter Nineteen

BELLA WAITED UNTIL Monday to answer Graham. She didn't know why he wanted to see her. The obvious reason—that he wanted to get back together—was one she was afraid to believe. Partly because if he did ask if they could get back together, she was afraid she'd say yes. And that would be a mistake. She still didn't know why he'd broken up with her in the first place. But if the reason was what she suspected, then taking him back was the last thing she should do.

She couldn't understand why he'd called things off. They'd been happy. She knew he had been too. They were growing closer. There was clearly no problem with the sex. They couldn't keep their hands off of each other. Yet a week after a wonderful weekend together, he'd broken her heart.

If he didn't want to get back together then what the hell did he want?

She texted him and told him she'd meet him at the coffee shop the next day during her lunch break. Or she said they could wait until the day after that if he was busy with work. Neutral turf. She would be in charge. She wouldn't have to see him at her place with her cat fawning all over him. At home, a place where he could kiss her and she'd melt like the fool she was. They'd be in a public place, which gave her an advantage. And the more advantages she had the better.

He chose the very next day. She wanted him to eat his heart out, so she chose her dress carefully.

It was a short, summery dress. A fun and flirty white with blue flowers, V-necked number that showed off her cleavage, though not in a sleazy way. Cute. Sexy. On her feet she wore strappy high-heeled wedges that she knew made her legs look good. She even wore makeup, more than her usual swipe of mascara and lipstick that was her normal work routine.

When she walked the three blocks to the coffee shop she was gratified to notice that she turned a few heads. Graham was already there when she arrived. *Why does he have to look so good? So damn tempting?*

He'd chosen a booth in the back to give them an illusion of privacy, she imagined. He stood and greeted her. "Thanks for seeing me, Bella. You look great."

"Thanks," she said shortly, sitting down across from him. "What did you want to see me about?"

"Can I get you a coffee or something to eat?" He had a cup in front of him. She loved the smell of coffee but to her this was not a simple chat.

"No, thanks."

"How have you been, Bella?"

"Busy. I don't have a lot of time. Why don't you get to the point?"

He looked disconcerted at that comment. "I've missed you."

"Your choice," she said.

"I know. Believe me, I'm totally aware of that. It didn't take long to realize I'd made a huge mistake."

"Really? You couldn't prove it by me. It's been over three weeks since we broke up. You haven't tried to see me until now. You haven't called. You've mostly treated me as if I didn't exist."

He flushed. "I realized my mistake quickly, but I didn't want to admit it. But I've missed you more every day we've been apart."

She raised her eyebrows. "You do sincerity very well." Be strong, she told herself. He doesn't mean it.

"It's not an act, Bella. I miss you. I miss us. Is there any way you can forgive me?"

She stared at him. He still hadn't said why he'd broken up with her. God, was he really that clueless? Apparently he was. "Yes, I can forgive you."

"You can? That's great! Does that mean we can get back together?"

"No." Oh, *hell*, no.

"But—" He looked completely shocked. "I don't understand. You said you could forgive me."

"I do forgive you. But there's no way I want to open myself up to getting hurt again like you hurt me."

"Damn it, Bella. I was a jerk. I'm sorry. You can't imagine how sorry I am. But I won't hurt you again."

"You can't promise that."

"We said we didn't want to get serious. But we did. You have to admit we did."

She shrugged.

"And we never discussed what to do if that happened."

"No, that's true. But we were getting along. Getting closer. I was even—" She checked herself before she finished the sentence. *I was even falling in love with you.* "Out of the blue, you called it off. For no reason. Or at least, no reason that you told me. Other than you 'needed space.' Which is, in my opinion, a pretty piss-poor reason."

"I was stupid. I've admitted that. I was afraid I was getting in too deep. So I pulled back."

She scoffed. "Oh, my God, Graham, can't you do better than that?"

"It's the truth."

"That's what every man says when he breaks up with a woman. It's rarely the real reason."

"It is this time." She simply looked at him. "What can I do to prove you can trust me?"

Tell me why you did it, for one thing. The real reason. Not the bullshit one. "I don't think there's anything you can do." Intent on leaving before she broke down in tears, she got up. "Goodbye, Graham." She walked out the door without a backward glance. And somehow managed to make it to the shop and run into the back before the tears came.

><

DAMN IT, SHE had an appointment. She'd glimpsed Joey

waiting for her as she ran by. She should have known better than to agree to meet Graham in the middle of a workday. Well, she couldn't stay back here and cry when her friend was waiting for her to do her hair.

Forgetting her makeup, she splashed water on her face. Then she had to repair that, so she wound up taking off the eye makeup rather than having black mascara all over her face. She looked in the mirror and shuddered. Her hair was plain blonde today and now she looked totally washed out. Oh, well, couldn't be helped. She blew her nose, slapped on lipstick and went to her station.

"Hi, Joey. Sorry I'm late."

"That's okay. What's wrong, Bella?"

"Nothing. I'm fine. So what are we doing today? You don't need your streak dyed. Unless you want to change the color?"

"No, I like the red. I wanted a hair trim but..." Her voice trailed off and she studied Bella in the mirror with a look that made her want to squirm.

It must be the librarian thing.

Bella plastered on her best fake smile. "How much do you want trimmed? Didn't we just recently trim it?"

"No offense, girlfriend, but you don't look in any shape to be using scissors. What in the world is wrong? Is it Graham? Did he do something else to upset you?"

Joey knew all about her and Graham breaking up. Not long after she'd told Delilah, she'd told Joey.

"I just came back from seeing him. But I'm fine. Really." Damn it, why did even thinking about the man make her want to cry?

"Bullshit," Joey said, getting up.

That comment coming from the quiet librarian let Bella know she was serious and wasn't about to let it drop.

"Come with me." Joey grabbed her arm and propelled her into the break room. "Sit down," Joey told her sternly. Bella sat and so did Joey. "Now tell me what happened."

"He said—he wants to get back together."

"But I thought you still loved him? Why are you crying?"

"Because I said no."

Joey got up to get a tissue and gave it to her. "Why?"

Bella told her about the entire conversation. That she'd forgiven him but said they weren't getting back together.

"Why? If you love him and he loves you—"

"He didn't say he loved me. He still won't even tell me why he broke up with me."

"No reason at all? That doesn't sound reasonable."

"Oh, he gave me a reason. A really lame one. We were getting too close. Too serious. So he pulled back. If I had a nickel for every time a man said that to break up with someone, I'd be as rich as Bill Gates."

Joey sat down again. "You're not going to like this, but...maybe he meant it."

"Meant what? That we were getting too close and that's why he bailed?"

"It's a reason. A stupid one, but a reason. And you both agreed you didn't want to be serious."

"Don't remind me," she said glumly.

"He's got an ex-wife. That could have made him commitment-shy."

Bella remembered what he'd said about his ex. She'd cheated on him. Because, she said, he was gone too much. He didn't pay enough attention to her, according to the ex. "I'm not like her. He should know that. Do I look like some clingy woman who can't be alone? Who needs a man to constantly be at her beck and call?"

Joey laughed. "No, Bella, that's not you."

"Well, according to him, that was his ex-wife."

"What are you going to do?"

"That's up to Graham. I told him I didn't think there was anything he could do to prove I could trust him. But I *didn't* say there was no way he could ever convince me to trust him again."

"Yes, but he's a man. Do you honestly think he'll figure that out?"

"I don't know. But if he really does want to get back together, he'll figure something out."

Chapter Twenty

AFTER GRAHAM LEFT the coffee shop, he called Spencer and said, "Meet me at the Saloon after work." He hung up, not even waiting for an answer. If his little brother knew what was good for him, he'd show. Sure enough, Spencer got there not long after Graham did. Looking irritated, which cheered Graham up.

"All right, I'm here," Spencer said, slapping his beer down on the table. "The least you could have done was get me a beer."

Graham ignored that. "I took your advice about Bella."

"Good. What happened?"

"Remind me not to listen to you again. I wasn't sure she would even see me at first. I texted her and asked if I could see her. She said she'd think about it. Can you believe that? She'd *think* about it." He was still annoyed at that.

Spencer laughed. "Sounds like she was pissed."

"Yeah. Anyway, she texted me three days later—three freaking days—and told me she'd meet me at the coffee shop."

Spencer laughed again. "Oh, man, I wish I could have seen your face. Did you meet her?"

"Yeah." Graham shrugged. "What other choice did I have?"

"None, if you wanted to see her."

"So I meet her at the damn coffee shop." She'd looked amazing. He wondered again why in the hell he'd broken up with her. "I told her I made a mistake and I wanted to get back together."

"What did she say?" He drank some of his beer.

"She said no."

"No? Just…no?"

"Apparently she doesn't trust me not to hurt her again. I asked her what I could do to prove to her that she could trust me and she said she didn't know that there was anything I could do."

Spencer started laughing for the third time. Big, deep belly laughs.

"What the hell are you laughing at? Did you hear what I said?"

"I heard. My God, this is priceless. You've never had to work at it before. Women have always fallen into your lap. You've finally met one who won't."

"Women don't 'fall into my lap.' That's ridiculous."

"Is it? Name me one woman who made you work to get them to go out with you."

"There were plenty."

Spencer raised his brows. "Name one."

Damn it, he couldn't. "You're not helping. What am I supposed to do now?"

"If you really want her—"

"I do. I'm in love with her."

"Really in love with her or just in lust?"

"Really in love. Damn it."

"Did you try telling her that?

"No. She wasn't interested."

"Charm her. Show her you care."

"How? I'm not even sure she'll see me again."

"My God, man. Do I have to do everything? She will. If you approach her right."

"How do I do that? Buy her things? I don't think she'll care about that. Money doesn't impress her."

"It's not how expensive the gift is. It's how thoughtful."

Thoughtful? "What does that mean?"

"What does she like? What's important to her? Get her a movie, or a book, or a song that will mean something to her. Does she like flowers? They're usually a good choice. But don't just send the flowers. Include something else with them. Make them mean you actually thought about what you're giving her."

Graham stared at him. "How do you know this shit?"

"I listen to women talk. You'd be surprised how much I hear on the job. People, especially women, like to talk to me. I have a trustworthy face."

"Trustworthy? More like vacuous."

"Now, now. Be nice or I won't help you."

"You already helped me and look how that turned out."

"Hey, it's not my fault you screwed it up. Go think about what I told you. You're supposedly bright. Figure out what she'll like and do it."

By the following day Bella had regained—well, almost—her customary attitude. She pushed Graham out of her mind as much as she was able and took Abby and herself off to work.

Bella was patiently waiting for Clara Perkins to decide what color she wanted her hair—today it was between turquoise and hot pink—when a delivery arrived from Krauss Blooms, the local florist. The delivery girl, Caro Parker, brought a huge vase of purple hyacinths over to Bella, set the flowers down on her station countertop—the container barely fit—and handed her a note and a wrapped present.

Speechless, Bella simply goggled at it.

"Open it up, girl," Clara said. "We all are dying to know what's in it." She looked around the shop and said slyly, "We already know who sent them."

Bella opened the paper and read the typed note.

PURPLE HYACINTHS

MEAN

I'M SORRY AND PLEASE FORGIVE ME.

Beneath that it read, *The package is for Abby. Love, Graham*

Bella opened the package. Three small tinsel balls nestled inside. She walked over to the window where Abby lay and gave her the toys. Abby immediately began playing with them.

"Well?" Clara said. "What does he say, girl?"

Bella handed the note to Clara. Clara read it aloud to a chorus of sighs. "You have to forgive him now," Amber, the esthetician, said.

She wasn't quite ready to forgive him but he'd definitely softened her up.

Bella called him when she got home. "Abby loves the tinsel balls."

"I'm glad. What does Abby's mom think about the flowers?"

She smiled. "They're beautiful. Thank you."

"I mean it, Bella. I'm so sorry."

"Graham, I—"

"I understand. You're not ready. I'll talk to you soon," he said, and hung up.

What am I supposed to do now?

The following day another delivery came. Daffodils this time. Along with a small package. She opened the note.

DAFFODILS

MEAN

NEW BEGINNINGS

Below that it read, *The package is for Abby. Love, Graham*

Bella opened the package and found a catnip squeaky mouse. She took it over to Abby, who, of course, loved it.

"You'd have me take him back right now, wouldn't you?" Bella asked her cat.

Delilah, who had come in for a trim, said, "You might not have forgiven him but Abby sure has. What does the

EVE GADDY

note say?"

Bella handed Delilah the note, prepared for the inevitable reaction. Delilah read it aloud. Just as Bella had expected, a chorus of sighs went up.

Patting her chest over her heart, Amber asked, "When are you going to put him out of his misery?"

"I don't know." Was she being too much of a hard-ass? Maybe. But she still wasn't sure that Graham wouldn't hurt her again. She still wasn't sure of his feelings. Or maybe it was just that she was afraid to trust that those feelings would last.

She called him again that night to thank him for the flowers and Abby's toy.

"You're welcome. Does Abby like the mouse?"

"Of course. It's got catnip in it."

"The clerk at the pet store said cats love catnip. The message with the flowers is a little misleading, though."

"You don't want new beginnings?"

"Not exactly. What I want is to never have broken up with you and caused you pain. What I want is not to have been such a dumbass."

Bella couldn't help laughing. "I want that too. But we can't change the past."

"No, but we can change the future. If you want to, that is."

He hung up, not pushing her anymore. But damn, the flowers, the gifts for Abby, when she talked to him, all those things were softening her up. Just like he intended.

When she went to work the day after that, she thought

for sure Graham wouldn't send more flowers. She thought he might do something else, but she was wrong. Caro came in with another vase of beautiful flowers. Blue irises. And a fairly large package.

BLUE IRISES
MEAN
HOPE

Below it he'd written, *Hoping you remember all the good times we had. The package is for Abby. Love, Graham*

Bella opened the package and found a toy box cat puzzle. She carried it over to Abby, who promptly went nuts over it.

"What does the note say?" someone called out.

"May I?" her client, a friend of Clara Perkins, asked, motioning to the note.

"Sure." Bella looked around. It seemed like there were an awful lot of people in the shop today. More so than usual. Many more. Good Lord, did everyone in town know about her and Graham?

Her client read the note aloud. Predictably, everyone sighed. Someone called out, "You'd better give that man another chance! If you don't I will!" Everyone in the shop erupted into laughter.

"I'll think about it," Bella said. But she was weakening.

❦

THAT EVENING, INSTEAD of calling Graham, Bella decided she needed to see him face to face. "Wish me luck," she told

Abby.

Abby looked at her with that inscrutable stare that cats have.

"No, I'm not sure what I expect to happen. Hell, I don't even know what I want to happen." Abby sniffed and went back to sleep.

Bella drove over to his apartment, parking on the street. She entered the lobby—spacious, well lit, and totally unlike her much older complex—and buzzed him.

"Yes?"

"It's Bella," she said, wondering if she was doing the right thing.

"I'll be right down."

He could have simply buzzed her in but instead he came to the lobby to ride up the elevator with her. He was barefoot, wearing jeans and an old T-shirt with a UT logo on it that fit snugly across his chest and arms. She wanted to drool but managed to get hold of herself.

"I should have called but I took a chance you'd be here."

"I'm glad I was. You look great, Bella."

"Thanks." No, she didn't. She had on a pair of jeans, ripped in the appropriate places, and a pink and white striped T-shirt that had seen better days. Her hair, streaked with pale pink and held with a clip, was piled up in a mess on the back of her head. But from the look in Graham's eyes, you'd think she was dressed to kill.

Other than that brief exchange they didn't speak until after he'd let them into his apartment. She'd been there before but she hadn't paid a lot of attention to the decor. She liked his apartment. It was a nice apartment anyway, since it was in the Millennial Village Apartments, and the complex had only been built a few years ago. He had a beautiful view of the river from his living room window. Someone had clearly taken the time to decorate the apartment in a style that suited him. Whether that was Graham or someone else's doing, she didn't know. It was a little spare, but not unwelcoming. A few things hung on the walls. One was a very lifelike painting of a red-tailed hawk diving for its prey. There was a landscape of the Hill Country in the spring with bluebonnets everywhere. And there was a metal wall hanging in varying shades of blue that looked like it was one of Gabe Walker's, a well-known metal artist who lived in Whiskey River.

"You like blue, don't you?"

He flashed a grin. "Guilty."

He had actual books, paperback and hardback, both on the shelves and lying around on his coffee table, side table and one on the kitchen counter. "Don't you read e-books?"

"Sure. But I like the feel of a real book too." He looked at her curiously for a minute. "You didn't come over to discuss my art or my reading habits."

"No, I wanted to thank you for the flowers. Again. They're beautiful. And Abby loves the presents you've been getting her."

"Good. I miss her."

"She misses you. And...so do I."

He let out a breath and took a step toward her. She went to him and let him gather her into his arms and laid her head on his chest. "You have no idea what it means to me for you to say that. God, Bella, I've missed you so much. I feel like it's been months since I held you."

"I know." She moved out of his arms and he let her go. She asked him what she'd wanted to know from the beginning. "Why did you break up with me, Graham?"

He sighed and ran a hand through his hair, making it messy and very appealing. "According to my brother Spencer, because I'm a chickenshit. He was right. I haven't fallen for a woman as hard as I did for you since my ex-wife. And you know how that turned out."

"So you were afraid of…what? That I'd turn out to be like your ex? That I'd want you to fawn all over me every minute?"

"No. But she wasn't like that at first, either."

"So you thought I'd change too."

"Not for long. Not after I got to know you."

"That wasn't why you broke up with me, though. Was it?"

"No. We were getting serious. Or I did, anyway. I started thinking about the future. About a future with you and what I'd feel like if I lost you."

"That makes sense," she said sarcastically.

"Bella, it almost killed me when I got divorced. And I realized I felt so much more for you than I had for my ex. It would make it that much worse to lose you."

"I don't understand. Why would you even think about that?"

He sighed. "Not long before we broke up, I had a case. A

man in his thirties with a heart problem so serious, he needed a new heart. I sent him and his wife to Houston to be evaluated for the transplant list. He left the room for a short time and she…she thanked me for what I'd done for him. When I hadn't done anything but arrange for him to go to the heart hospital in Houston.

"She told me he was the love of her life and she didn't know what she'd do if the worst happened. I had no real words of comfort for her. Trying to be upbeat yet realistic was impossible in this case. The best I could do was tell her that the hospital and doctors in Houston were the best there was and I was sure they'd do everything in their power to help him."

He lapsed into silence. "Was that true?" she asked.

"Yes. But there are no guarantees. Even if he was a good candidate for a transplant, there might not be a heart available for him in time."

"I still don't understand. You've lost patients before. You're bound to have had similar cases to this one before. What made this one so different?"

"This time I was in love with you. It's a lot easier to deal with that kind of thing when you're not in love and don't think you ever will be again. But I realized it didn't matter. All I'd done when I broke up with you was make myself miserable. It didn't make me love you any less."

"We could have worked this out earlier if you'd just talked to me. Been honest with me about your feelings."

"You're forgetting that I didn't know how you felt. You told me there wasn't anything I could do to get you back. I still don't know how you feel. Other than pissed at me."

"I'm not pissed anymore." But neither was she ready to admit she loved him. "I thought you'd broken up with me because you decided—or realized—I'm not your type."

"Not my type? What do you mean?"

"Fern said I would put your career at risk. I thought you believed that too."

"Why?"

"You never told me you were in the running for the chief of surgery position once Dr. Prior retires. I thought you'd decided that being involved with me would hold you back. And I worried that I would."

"You figured this out because of something Fern Nixon said? Fern?"

"You never even mentioned it. Why didn't you tell me?"

"Because it had no bearing on you and me. Besides, I'm not even totally sure I want it."

"Why wouldn't you? Isn't it an honor?"

"To an extent. It's also a lot more work. Paperwork. I'm not interested in having paperwork supersede my operating schedule." He shrugged. "I'm not going to worry about it. If it happens, great. If not, so what? It's not the end of the world. Did you really believe you could be a handicap to me and my career?"

"I didn't want to. At first, I blew it off. But then you broke up with me and you wouldn't really tell me why. And Fern got under my skin. I couldn't help wondering if she was right."

"Well, she's not. Bella, don't you know I'm crazy about

you?"

"No. I knew you liked me. I knew you liked the sex but when you broke up with me it was…out of the blue, to me at least. And I really didn't know what to think. I don't like feeling that way."

"God, I really did screw up." He went to her and put his hands on her arms, holding her gently and saying, "Bella, look at me."

She did, scanning his face, looking into his eyes.

"I love you, Bella. I love you so much. And I'm so, so sorry I hurt you." He kissed her lips, very gently. "I'm madly in love with you. And it scared the hell out of me for several reasons. I'm not exactly a good bet in the serious relationship department. The destruction of my marriage wasn't all my ex-wife's fault. I have to take responsibility for some of it."

"She cheated on you."

"Yes. But maybe she wouldn't have if I'd been different. More understanding, less completely obsessed with my work."

"That doesn't excuse her."

"No, but I've always felt guilty that I couldn't give her what she needed. I didn't want to fail again. Especially not with you. So I bailed before I could disappoint both of us."

"I wish you hadn't."

"So do I. But I can't change what I did; I can only resolve to learn from it. And what I learned is I really love you and while we can't guarantee the future we can take advantage of the now. I want you and hope with all my heart you can forgive me and take me back."

"Oh, Graham." How could she deny him when everything he said was exactly what she needed to hear? "I love you too."

Chapter Twenty-One

"DID YOU SAY—?" Graham broke off, afraid he'd imagined her last words.

"I love you."

"Thank God," he said, and kissed her. A kiss with all the pent-up longing he'd been denying for so long. Bella kissed him back and soon they were ripping at each other's clothes, desperate to reach bare skin. He pushed up her T-shirt and she pulled it off over her head and flung it aside. She slid her hands beneath his shirt, stroking his chest. He yanked it off and threw it aside.

They fumbled with each other's jeans. He undid hers and helped her peel them off, only taking his mouth off of hers for a moment. Bella had managed to unbutton his jeans and partially unzip them but he was so hard and ready for her she was having trouble getting them off.

He lifted her up so she could wrap her legs around him and headed for his bedroom. After letting her slide down his body—deliciously slowly—to stand beside the bed, he stripped off his jeans and boxers while Bella opened the drawer of the bedside table and pulled out a condom.

He took it from her, afraid if she touched him, he'd go

off like a rocket. Then he sat on the bed and she climbed on top. Their gazes locked as he held her hips and guided her until she was poised directly over his cock. She kissed him deeply and slid down onto him just as he thrust upward to bury himself to the hilt inside of her.

They both groaned and then she began to ride. Holding on to her hips with one hand, he used the other to fondle her breasts, to pluck at her stiffened nipples, driving her higher with each thrust.

He felt her feminine muscles tighten around him, her soft, wet heat push him closer to the edge. He heard her cry out his name as she shattered and his orgasm ripped through him and he spilled himself deep inside her.

They stayed locked together, just holding on to each other. After a while Bella got off of him and went to the bathroom. They traded places and he got rid of the condom. When he returned she was lying in bed and he slipped in beside her.

"I can't stay," she said. "I don't want to leave Abby all night."

"I know. I understand. But I don't want you to leave."

"You could come to my apartment."

He rose on his forearm to look down at her. Her hair was spread over his pillow, blonde and pink. He tangled his fingers in it. "It reminds me of cotton candy."

She looked puzzled. "What does?"

"Your hair. Soft. Pink. Pretty."

"Cotton candy is sticky."

Graham laughed. "Good point. Okay, not cotton candy.

Silk. Pink silk."

"That's better. Are you going to come over?"

"I would love to."

It took them quite a while to get dressed, since they had to stop and kiss often. But eventually they left his apartment and he followed her in his car, since he'd need it to go to work.

Once there, after he said hello to Abby, he took Bella to bed and made love to her again. But slowly this time. Touching and tasting every inch of her skin and then she pushed him onto his back and drove him mad with her lips and hands exploring his body. When he couldn't take any more, he flipped her onto her back and drove inside her. Her breath hitched and he pulled out and did it again. And again. He felt her muscles spasm, contracting with her orgasm until she pushed him over the edge and he came with a rush that nearly blew off the top of his head.

They didn't sleep much that night. They talked. Some. Made love. A lot. And part of the time they were both content just to hold each other. Graham couldn't remember being this happy...ever.

BELLA WOKE UP when she felt the bed give. She rolled over and saw Graham pulling on his jeans. "Are you leaving?"

"Sorry, I didn't mean to wake you."

"S'okay Do you have to go?"

"Yes." He pulled on his T-shirt. "Sorry but I have to—"

He broke off when she sat up and rubbed her eyes. Graham was standing stock-still, staring at her. Realizing she was naked, she gave him a slow smile. "Are you positive you have to go?"

He groaned and averted his eyes. "Don't tempt me. I have to make rounds, which means I have to go home and shower and change."

"You could shower here."

He shook his head regretfully. "No, I can't. Because then I'd get you to shower with me and we'd make love and I'd still have to go home and change and by then it would be noon before I made rounds. Besides, I have something I have to do this afternoon, so I need to get my work done early."

Bella laughed. "My, that was convoluted. All right, if you have to leave, you have to leave." She got out of bed, went to her dresser and opened a drawer, pulling out a T-shirt she often slept in. She slipped it on over her head and said, "There. Is that better?"

He groaned again. "Not even a little."

She looked down, then back up at him. "I'm covered up."

"Barely. And there's nothing beneath that shirt."

"I guess you'll just have to come over later."

He walked forward and pulled her into his arms. "I guess I will." Then he kissed her, a bone-meltingly hot kiss that pretty much made her forget her name. "Come lock up behind me."

"All right. I should be home around six."

"Great. I'll give you a call before I come over."

At the door he kissed her again. Rubbing his knuckles against her cheek, he said, "This is the first good morning I've had since we broke up."

"Me too." She pushed him out the door. "Go to work. We'll talk later."

"That too," he said with a wicked grin.

She shut the door behind him and sighed happily. She went to make coffee and dawdled over it, reliving the night before until she realized she was going to be late for work if she didn't get busy and stop daydreaming.

By the time Bella and Abby got to the shop she was only ten minutes late. The shop was more crowded than Bella could ever remember it being. "Y'all are going to be awfully disappointed when no flowers come."

"We have faith," Clara Perkins said. No, Clara didn't have an appointment but she'd come to the shop anyway and dared anyone to make her leave. If fact, there was more than one person in the shop who wasn't there for an appointment.

Oh, my God, surely they're not all here waiting for the flowers. If they were, she thought they were doomed to disappointment. Since she and Graham had made up, she wasn't expecting more flowers or presents.

Joey, who'd come in for the haircut she'd missed the other day, said, "I'll bet you a dollar Graham does something amazing today."

"He already did," she said, remembering the night before. "Ah-mazing."

"You slept with him!" Joey said in delight. "It's about time you forgave him."

"Say that a little louder. I don't think everyone heard

you," Bella said.

"Sorry," Joey said, but she didn't look in the least sorry. "But I'm so happy for you."

Shortly after that, while she was still trimming Joey's hair, a delivery person came in carrying a huge box. "This is for Abby Benson," he announced.

Bella laughed. "I'll have to take it for her."

"I don't know," the deliveryman said doubtfully. "I think I'm supposed to give it directly to Abby Benson."

"If you say so. She's in the window."

He looked to the window she pointed at. "That's a cat."

"Yes, she is. That's Abby Benson."

"Uh—"

Taking pity on him, Bella took the clipboard from him and signed next to Abby's name. "There. I'm sure it will be fine. I have a feeling I know who sent it."

Before he left he remembered to hand her a note. "What does it say?" Amber called out.

She read aloud, "For Abby, love, Graham."

"That's not very exciting," Amber complained.

"It's for Abby. She can't read anyway." Bella opened the box. "I'm going to need some help."

Joey got up and helped her pull out a very large scratching post with a perch on top. They carried it over to the window. Abby looked at it a bit suspiciously, but leapt down and sniffed it. Then she pawed at it. She must have realized what it was for because she began sharpening her claws.

"That's so sweet of him," Joey said.

They went back to Bella's station and Bella returned to trimming Joey's hair. "I'm pretty sure the show's over if y'all want to go home," she told the group at large. Clara didn't budge. Neither did anyone else. Bella sighed. "Fine, stay here all day. You're going to get hungry."

"We can order pizza," Amber said.

"I'll take up a collection," one of the other hairdressers said.

Bella rolled her eyes.

"I'm in," Joey said, laughing. "I'm always up for pizza."

The bell over the front door jangled again. Bella looked up and caught her breath.

"Looks like you were wrong," Joey said.

Graham walked toward her carrying a huge vase of red roses. So many she couldn't even count them. He wore jeans and a baby-blue button-down shirt and looked so good she wanted to eat him up. He set down the vase and smiled at her.

"I thought you had work to do," she said.

"I did. I finished it."

"Do the roses have a note to go with them?"

"Nope. I'm delivering the message in person."

"What do roses mean?"

"Red roses mean I love you."

He'd told her he loved her last night but for him to announce it here, in her shop, in front of half the town…her heart simply melted. Tears sprang to her eyes. "Oh, Graham. I love you, too." She started to throw her arms around him but he held her off.

"Not so fast." He pulled something from his pocket and got down on one knee.

Bella's heart thudded. "What are you doing?" she whispered.

He ignored her and took hold of her left hand. "Bella Benson, I love you. I am completely, totally, madly, crazy in love with you." He held out a beautiful diamond solitaire ring surrounded by smaller diamonds, in an old-fashioned platinum setting. "Will you marry me, Bella?"

She couldn't breathe. He'd literally taken her breath away. She managed a shaky, "Graham."

"Bella."

She stared at him, still wondering if she'd heard him correctly or she was hallucinating. "I'm really starting to worry here," he said, but his eyes were laughing.

She let out her breath. "Yes. Yes, I'll marry you."

He slipped the ring on her finger, then rose and swept her into his arms. "Soon," he said, and kissed her.

She vaguely heard applause and whistles but Graham was kissing her senseless and it was all she could do to hold on and kiss him back. When he finally let her up for air, he scooped her up in his arms. "Excuse us," he said and started toward the back.

"Wait," Bella said, suddenly remembering Joey. "I was in the middle of trimming Joey's hair."

He started to put her down, but Joey waved them away. "I'll start a new trend. I'm calling it the 'Bella got engaged' cut."

Everyone laughed. "I owe you," Bella said over Graham's shoulder as he carried her off.

"Dang right you do," Joey said.

The End

Love the town of Last Stand, Texas? Stay awhile. Where the women are feisty, the men are sexy and the romance is hotter than ever.

Last Stand, Texas

Heart of the Texas Doctor by Eve Gaddy

Her Texas Ex by Katherine Garbera

The Lone Star Lawman by Justine Davis

A Son for the Texas Cowboy by Sinclair Jayne

The Perfect Catch by Joanne Rock

Available now at your favorite online retailer!

Devil's Rock at Whiskey River

Book 1: *Rebel Pilot, Texas Doctor*

Book 2: *His Best Friend's Sister*

Book 3: *No Ordinary Texas Billionaire*

Available now at your favorite online retailer!

About the Author

Eve Gaddy is the best-selling award-winning author of more than seventeen novels. Her books have won and been nominated for awards from Romantic Times, Golden Quill, Bookseller's Best, Holt Medallion, Texas Gold, Daphne Du Maurier and more. She was nominated for a Romantic Times Career Achievement Award for Innovative Series romance as well as winning the 2008 Romantic Times Career Achievement award for Series Storyteller of the year. Eve's books have sold over a million copies worldwide and been published in many foreign countries. Eve lives in East Texas with her husband of many years.

Thank you for reading

Heart of the Texas Doctor

If you enjoyed this book, you can find more from all our great authors at TulePublishing.com, or from your favorite online retailer.

TULE
PUBLISHING

Made in the USA
Columbia, SC
28 October 2021